Her eyes narrowed. "I'm going to try to make the best of this. I expect you to do the same."

"How do you suppose we go about doing that?"

"I think we should agree to avoid each other whenever humanly possible. After this week, we never have to see each other again."

A corner of his mouth twitched but he held the smile inside. "Sounds like a good idea."

She narrowed her eyes at him. "So that's it?"

"Sure." It did sound like a good idea. For *her.* But the way he saw it, he was long overdue for a little payback. Some good old-fashioned revenge.

If keeping his distance was what she really wanted, for the next week he would be stuck to that woman like glue.

Dear Reader,

As a writer, I find nothing more entertaining than taking two characters with a long, complicated history, sticking them together for a week and watching while they sort everything out. This time I got a bit more than I bargained for.

I usually get to know my hero and heroine early on in the plotting process, but I began writing this book knowing very little about Ivy and Dillon. They were...elusive.

The truth is, I dragged them both into the story kicking and screaming. From the very first line in chapter one to the last line of the final chapter, these two gave me a hard time. They just wouldn't *listen*. If I said go left, they went right. If I told them to slow down, they rushed forward. Had they been physically sitting in my office I would have smacked them both upside the head!

"Do things my way and this will be so much easier," I begged them repeatedly, but if they couldn't trust each other, they sure weren't going to trust me. They didn't want to be there, and they fought me tooth and nail. But as frustrating as it could be at times (pretty much every time I sat down at the keyboard), they kept things interesting. They made me want to *fight* for them. I laughed and cried and learned to love these two stubborn people.

I hope you enjoy their journey as much as I did.

Michelle

MICHELLE CELMER

BEST MAN'S CONQUEST

Published by Silhouette Books

America's Publisher of Contemporary Romance

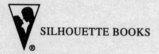

SILHOUETTE BOOKS

ISBN-13: 978-0-373-76799-1
ISBN-10:   0-373-76799-4

BEST MAN'S CONQUEST

Visit Silhouette Books at www.eHarlequin.com

Printed in U.S.A.

MICHELLE CELMER

lives in a southeastern Michigan zoo. Well, okay, it's really a house, but with three teenagers, three dogs, three cats (are you seeing a pattern here?) and a fifty-gallon tank full of various marine life, sometimes it feels like a zoo. It's rarely quiet, seldom clean, and between after-school jobs, various extracurricular activities and band practice, getting everyone home at the same time to share a meal is next to impossible.

You can often find Michelle locked in her office, writing her heart out and loving the fact that she doesn't have to leave the house to go to work, or even change out of her pajamas.

Michelle loves to hear from her readers. Drop her a line at P.O. Box 300, Clawson, MI 48017, or visit her Web site at www.michellecelmer.com.

I dedicate this work to my future Great Niece or Nephew, who will make his or her appearance at roughly the same time as this book. You have five brothers, so naturally your mommy is hoping for a girl.

Try to work on that okay?

One

Ivy Madison was not a violent person, but as the "surprise" man she'd been hearing about for the past three months—the one who looked disturbingly similar to her gazillionaire ex-husband—unfolded his long, lean body from the backseat of the limo, she quietly began plotting her cousin Deidre's murder.

No, it couldn't possibly be him.

Blake, Deidre's fiancé, was supposed to be off

picking up the best man from the airport. There was
no way that the surprise Deidre had repeatedly
enticed her with, the mystery best man Ivy was just
going to *love,* was Dillon Marshal! Never in a million
years would Deidre expect Ivy to stand up in a
wedding, much less spend the week before the
ceremony in the Mexican villa, with the biggest
mistake who had ever walked in, then walked back
out of, her life.

Would she?

Maybe the surprise was that the best man only looked
like Dillon. Yeah, that was probably it. They would have
a good laugh, then Ivy could relax and enjoy the first
real vacation since the release of her book.

It was just one of those weird, quirky coincidences.

The man who couldn't possibly be her ex slipped off
his Ray-Bans, revealing a familiar pair of heavy-lidded,
come-hither, steel-blue bedroom eyes. Eyes that had been
known to melt her with a mere glance, reduce her knees
to mashed potatoes and her head to scrambled eggs.

Oh shi—

A blast of emotions tore through her insides with the
velocity of a tropical storm, misfiring the synapses in
her brain and tangling her intestines into knots.

She turned from the front window and looked to her
cousin for an explanation. For an assurance that there
was no way the man standing in the driveway was who
he looked like.

Deidre flashed her a look seeped in guilt and offered
a weak, "Surprise."

Oh, no.

Ivy's heart slid down from her chest, weaved around her internal organs and settled just north of her ovaries.

Her knees felt as if they might give out, and the bagel she'd had for breakfast was in danger of making a repeat performance all over the southwestern-theme rug. This could not be happening. There was a damned good reason she'd spent the last decade avoiding Dillon.

Feeling woozy, she lowered herself onto the couch. She glanced out the window and saw that men were at the back of the limo now, collecting Dillon's luggage. Soon they would be coming inside.

Her stomach launched into an Olympic-caliber backflip with a triple twist.

Deidre sat down on the opposite end of the couch, far enough away to hopefully avoid any flying fists. "I know you probably want to kill me right now, but I can explain."

Oh, yeah, she definitely had to die. And it would be slow and painful. Stung to death by African bees, or drained by a million leeches. "Deidre, what did you do?"

"I have a very good explanation."

There was no good explanation. And there was only one thing Ivy could do. She needed to grab her things, slip out the back, and catch the next flight back to Texas.

She made a mental list of her belongings and tried to estimate how long it would take to shove them back into her bag.

Oh, to hell with her clothes. She had plenty more back home. All she really needed was her laptop and purse. She could grab them both and be out the back door in two minutes. Dillon would never be the wiser. Unless…

Oh, no, she wouldn't have. "This was a surprise for him, too, right?"

Deidre clamped her bottom lip between her teeth, eyes pinned in her lap, and Ivy felt the bagel creeping farther up her throat.

"Deidre, *honey,* tell me he doesn't know I'm here."

The color leached from her cheeks.

"Deidre?"

"He knows."

Wonderful. Just *freaking* fantastic.

That meant running was not an option. No way she could let Dillon know he'd scared her off. Even worse, he'd had time to prepare for this. He would do and say all the right things.

Oh, who was she kidding? Dillon was not the type of guy who needed to prepare.

Oh boy, she was in big trouble.

The front door opened, and Ivy's heart sped up triple time. With an excited squeal Deidre dashed from the room to greet them, leaving Ivy alone.

Traitor.

She wasn't ready for this. Had she not been forced, she didn't know if she would have *ever* been ready to face Dillon again. Too much bad blood. Too many regrets.

She heard voices from the other room, enthusiastic greetings and the unmistakable hum of Dillon's deep, easy voice. Her heart started going berserk in her chest.

No matter what, she could not let that man see her this rattled.

She rose from the couch on rubbery legs and turned to look out the window at the taillights of the limo as it pulled down the driveway. Something was said about taking the luggage to the bedroom, then she heard the sound of footsteps on the stairs—more than one set. She closed her eyes and clung to the breath in her lungs until her head began to swim from lack of oxygen, praying Deidre was showing Dillon up to his room and she could put off a little longer the inevitable confrontation.

She needed time to prepare. Ten or fifteen minutes. Or a week.

For several long seconds the house was still and silent. She exhaled slowly, felt her heart rate returning to a somewhat normal pace, and sucked in a fresh breath.

Then a familiar feeling—something warm and complicated and unpredictable—poured over her. It soaked through her clothes and drenched her skin and she knew without turning that Dillon was in the room. She could feel his presence, the pressure of his gaze on her back, like some creepy sixth sense.

Goose bumps broke out across her arms, and the fine hairs on her neck started to shiver.

Oh, boy, here we go.

Gathering every scrap of courage she could dredge up, she fixed what she hoped was a disinterested look on her face and turned to confront a past that up until today she thought she'd seen the last of. The man recently dubbed one of the country's most eligible bachelors.

He leaned in the arched doorway, arms folded over his chest. Arms that somehow managed to appear muscular and lean at the same time, a chest wide enough to impress but not overpower. Memories of those arms around her, her cheek pressed to that warm, solid chest breathing in the clean, subtle scent of his aftershave, rushed up to choke the air from her lungs.

In faded blue jeans, a white T-shirt and cowboy boots, the billionaire oil king looked just as he had in college. Yet there was an air of authority and importance that emanated from inside him, from every pore. An arrogance that said he knew exactly what he wanted and he wasn't afraid to go after it, and pity the person who dared get in his way.

Beginning with her pink-tipped toes, his eyes embarked on a leisurely journey, working their way up her body. Slowly they climbed, no shame, no apology, as if he had every right to be mentally undressing her.

Over her hips, across her mostly flat stomach…

She clasped her hands behind her back, so he wouldn't see them tremble. What was wrong with her? She was no longer the naive, sheltered girl who had been swept away by a trust-fund rebel. She was a strong, self-confident professional. She had co-written the definitive guide on divorce for the modern woman. She was a *New York Times* bestselling author, for cripes' sake. She could handle Dillon Marshall.

She hoped.

He finally reached her breasts and took his sweet ole time, caressing them with his eyes. She felt the tips tingle and tighten against her will. The urge to cross her arms over her chest was almost unbearable, but she wouldn't give him the satisfaction.

This inspection, this violation, was all a part of the game he played.

She narrowed her eyes and raised her chin to a don't-even-mess-with-me angle. When he finally reached her face, his eyes locked on hers and held, and one corner of his mouth tipped up in a familiar, cocky smile.

He shook his head, eyes simmering with male appreciation. "Damn, darlin', you look good enough to eat."

If looks could kill, Dillon would be knocking at the pearly gates. His ex-wife's whiskey-colored eyes impaled him like razor-sharp daggers.

Talk about a blast from the past. It was the same look she'd given him ten years ago, the day she walked out on him.

Though the particulars of that morning were still fuzzy, he remembered stumbling in stinking drunk at 7:00 a.m. after an all-nighter with his buddies. His third all-nighter that week…and it had been only Wednesday. He'd tried to coax her into bed, to show her how sorry he was—hell, it had worked before—and she'd lobbed an empty beer bottle at his head.

Lucky for him that her aim had been as bad as her temper.

But damn, did she look good now—tall and willowy and soft around the edges. The kind of pretty that crept up on a man slowly, then dug its claws in deep and held on.

Too bad she was a major pain in the behind.

He turned up the charm on his smile, knowing it would irritate the hell out of her, since that in large part was the motivation for this trip. He intended to make her suffer. "What, no kiss?"

Sure enough, that telltale little crease formed between her eyebrows. She always had taken life too seriously. He used to admire her confidence, her determination. The woman knew exactly what she wanted, and she hadn't been afraid to go after it. Too bad she'd never learned how to have fun. He'd tried his best to teach her, to loosen her up, and what had it gotten him?

A lot of grief.

It would be that much more satisfying when he finally broke her spirit.

"You don't look happy to see me," he said.

Her eyes narrowed, like maybe she thought that if she concentrated hard enough she could wish him out of existence.

"Oh, right, you still think I'm a…now, how did you word it in that little book of yours?" He scratched his chin thoughtfully. "Something to the effect of me being a self-centered, pigheaded horse's ass?"

Her chin rose in that familiar, stubborn tilt. "Not once did I use your name in that *little* book, so you can't say one way or the other who I was referring to."

She might not have used his name, but the implication had been more than clear.

Clear to him.

Clear to his family and friends.

And clear to the millions of women who had flocked to the bookstore to get their hands on the new must-read self-help guide.

Nearly every negative little story and anecdote she'd included in the text had been plucked right out of their marriage. Talk about social devastation. The class of woman he normally dated wouldn't give him the time of day, and the women who would, the morbidly curious and monetarily motivated, he wouldn't wish on his worst enemy.

"Besides, it was self-*absorbed* and *bull*headed," Ivy added. "And I never used the term horse's ass. Even though you were one."

He flattened a hand across the left side of his chest. "Darlin', you're breakin' my heart."

"Look, you can cut the *good ole boy* crap. I don't imagine you're any happier than I am about being stuck together for a whole week."

It was just like her to cut through the bull and get right to the point. And as usual, she was wrong. He couldn't be happier.

"For Deidre and Blake's sake, I'm going to try to make the best of it," she continued in that master-of-the-universe tone. "I expect you to do the same."

He just bet she did. Was she under the impression they were going to pick up where they left off? With her issuing orders?

Had she forgotten that he didn't take orders from anyone?

"How do you s'pose we go about doing that?" he asked in the same *good ole boy* twang, since it clearly annoyed her.

"I think we should agree to avoid each other whenever humanly possible. I'll stay out of your way and you stay out of mine. After this week, we never have to see each other again."

The *never seeing each other again* part sounded just fine to him. But that was only a fraction of the good news. He'd been looking for a way to irritate her, to make her as miserable as humanly possible, and she'd just served it up on a silver platter.

The worst thing he could do to a control freak like Ivy was take away her control.

A corner of his mouth twitched, but he held the smile inside. He pretended to give her demand some thought, then gave her a solemn nod. "Sounds like a good idea."

She narrowed her eyes at him. "So that's it?"

"Sure." It did sound like a good idea. For *her*. That didn't mean *he* had any intention of doing it.

She had no idea the flack his family had taken after her book was released. Call it childish and immature—hell, he'd been called worse—but the way he saw it, he was long overdue for a little payback. Some good old-fashioned revenge.

If keeping his distance was what she really wanted, for the next week he would be stuck to that woman like glue.

Two

Feeling helpless, hopeless? Stand up and take control! Show that man who's boss.
—excerpt from *The Modern Woman's Guide to Divorce (And the Joy of Staying Single)*

Ivy sat outside on the private balcony of her bedroom, at the cute little wrought-iron patio set, reading the novel she'd started on the plane. The sun felt warm on her skin, and a damp, salty ocean breeze flipped the ends of her ponytail.

What better place to relax? To kick back and put her feet up? Yet she was so tense she'd read the same paragraph half a dozen times and still had no idea what it said.

She marked her page and set the book down, rubbing

at the beginnings of a headache in her temples. This was supposed to be a vacation. It was supposed to be fun.

She heard her bedroom door open, and her cousin called to her. "Are you in here?"

Ivy looked at her watch. It had taken Deidre a full hour to work up the courage to face her again.

"I'm out here," she said.

Several seconds passed, then she heard Deidre behind her. "Are you mad at me?"

Mad?

Mad didn't scratch the surface of what she was feeling. She felt hurt and betrayed and *humiliated.* They were supposed to be best friends. The sister neither had ever had.

A *team.*

How could Deidre pull a stunt like this? How could she lie by omission?

She turned to her cousin. Deidre stood in the bedroom doorway wringing the color from her hands, looking like the poster girl for guilt and remorse.

She'd been a nervous wreck for weeks, sure that at any moment Blake would come to his senses and finally accept the truth. Deidre, with a family history of obesity and bad skin, would never be a supermodel. Then he would undoubtedly start listening when his parents and brothers assured him that, for all his money and family connections, he could do much better.

Deidre also had what looked like a smear of chocolate in the corner of her mouth. Just that morning Ivy had confiscated a six-pack of chocolate bars and a half-empty box of Ding Dongs from Deidre's bedroom. She didn't want to venture a guess as to how much weight

Deidre had gained back in the last month or so, but a few more pounds and she would look like an overstuffed sausage in her ten-thousand-dollar designer wedding gown. Even worse was the random acne that had begun to spring up on her chin. Which of course only made her more upset, and more likely to stuff her face with junk.

She'd been a neurotic mess for weeks. Still, that didn't excuse what she had done.

Ivy concentrated on keeping her voice calm and rational. "How could you do this to me?"

"I'm so sorry. But I knew if I told you, you wouldn't have come. Without you as my maid of honor, it would ruin *everything*."

Deidre was one of those women who had begun planning her wedding the instant she left the womb. She'd accumulated a ceiling-high stockpile of bridal magazines and catalogs by the fifth grade.

After a few miserably failed false starts, she had finally snagged Mr. Right. Ivy got the feeling Deidre saw this as her last chance and that, if everything didn't go exactly as planned, she was destined to spend the rest of her life alone and childless and die a bitter spinster.

"I told you the best man was a buddy from college, and you knew he and Blake went to school together."

Ivy knew they had shared an apartment at Harvard, until Dillon had been expelled, that is, but she hadn't known they were that close. Her and Dillon's quickie Vegas wedding had been too last-minute for a best man or maid of honor.

Or a cake.

Or even a wedding dress.

It had been more of a *we'll show them* when their parents had tried to interfere in their relationship. Proving that not only is love blind, it's downright idiotic.

The sad truth is, she and Dillon had barely known each other when they'd gotten married. Out of bed, anyway. Only after their vows had she realized her mistake.

The day after.

"I know you probably won't believe this," Deidre said, "but Dillon has changed."

"You're right. I don't believe it." Men like Dillon never changed. Not deep down, where it counted.

"Maybe it's time you…" Deidre paused, her lip clamped between her teeth again.

"It's time I what?"

She shrugged. "Maybe…get past it."

"Get past what?"

"What I mean is, maybe it's time you…forgive him."

Forgive him?

Was Deidre joking? Had the wedding jitters short-circuited her brain? Had she forgotten what Dillon had put her through?

Did a woman ever get past having her heart stomped on and filleted into a million pieces? Did she forget losing an academic grant, being tossed out of college and having her reputation decimated?

And how did you forgive someone who showed no remorse? Someone who sat back and watched with a smile on his face while her world fell apart? A man who had promised to love and honor her until death? "What Dillon did to me was unforgivable and you know it."

Deidre lowered herself into the chair beside Ivy's, a look of genuine concern on her face. "I just hate to see you so unhappy."

Her words nearly knocked Ivy out of her chair. "What are you talking about? My book is selling millions, my private practice is flourishing. Why in the world would I be unhappy?"

"You're the psychologist. You tell me."

Ivy had everything she'd ever dreamed of. A good career and an impressive stock portfolio. Personal and financial independence.

She was not unhappy. In fact, she was freaking ecstatic. "For your information, I am very happy with my life."

"When was the last time you were in a committed relationship? When was the last time you had sex? Hell, when was the last time you were on a date?"

"I don't need a man to complete me." The words spilled from her mouth automatically. It was her mantra, the basis for her book. The only constant in her life.

"Maybe not, but they sure can be fun to have around."

And so not worth the hassle. She had her career and her friends. That was enough. For now. "Setting me up like this has put me in a terrible position. Considering all the people who will be at the wedding Saturday, it's bound to get out that I spent a week in Mexico with my ex. You know how brutal the media can be. What if they start spreading rumors that we're getting back together? What do you think that will do to my reputation?"

"I guess I never thought about it like that." Deidre's lower lip began to quiver and tears hovered just inside her eyelids. "I was only trying to help. If you want to leave, I understand."

Ivy sighed. As mad as she was at her cousin, deep down she knew her intentions were pure. Deidre didn't have a vindictive bone in her body. If she said she was trying to help, it was the truth, and it was executed out of love and concern.

Oh, hell.

She reached over and squeezed Deidre's fisted hands. "I'm not going anywhere. This is the most important week of your life, and I wouldn't miss it for anything."

The tears spilled over onto Deidre's cheeks and rolled down, leaving wet dots on the front of her shirt. "Thank you."

"Besides, Dillon and I talked, and we've reached somewhat of an agreement. I'll avoid him and he'll avoid me." She gave Deidre's hands a reassuring squeeze and forced a smile. "Really, how bad could it be?"

It could be bad, Ivy realized fifteen minutes later after Deidre left to see about dinner. Really bad.

She experienced the same eerie, familiar feeling as she had downstairs when Dillon had entered the room, and she looked up to find him a stone's throw away, leaning on the edge of his own balcony on the opposite end of the house. His eyes were on her, steady and intense, as if he was biding his time, just waiting for her to notice him there.

"Howdy!" he called, wiggling his fingers in a casual, friendly, good-ole-boy wave. He looked out across the ocean, his chest expanding beneath his T-shirt as he drew in a long, deep breath. "Hell of a view, isn't it?"

Oh, yes it is, she agreed silently, her eyes wandering over his solid frame. And she could feel it coming on, that little shimmy thing her heart did whenever he was near.

Here it comes…

No, no, no!

She lowered her eyes back to her book. Don't look at him. Don't encourage him in any way. Maybe he would take the hint and leave her alone.

He didn't.

"Whatcha' doin'?"

"Reading," she answered, not looking up from the page. Maybe if she kept her answers short and succinct he would get a clue. He would realize she wanted him to leave her alone. Like he promised he would.

He didn't.

She could still feel his eyes on her, feel him watching. Goose bumps shivered across her skin, and she felt fidgety and uncomfortable.

Ignore him and he'll lose interest, she assured herself. Keep reading and he'll get bored and go away. But she could feel her anxiety level climbing again. Her foot had begun to tap, the way it always did when she was nervous, and she was grinding her teeth.

She forced herself to relax.

"Good book?" He used a tone that suggested he was making friendly conversation. Maybe to break the ice, so the situation would be a bit less awkward.

He was wasting his time. The only conversation she was interested in having with him was the nonexistent kind. She didn't want to break the ice, and she had no desire to make things less awkward.

She just wanted him to go away.

There was also the distinct possibility that, despite his promise to leave her alone, he was doing this to annoy her.

Either way, she was beginning to feel like a specimen under a microscope.

She took several deep, cleansing breaths, tried to concentrate on her book and not on the man staring at her.

After a few very long, tense moments he said, "Must be a good book."

"It is." Up until a few minutes ago, anyway. Now, as she tried to focus on the small print, the words ran together in a nonsensical jumble. Was a few minutes of peace really too much to ask for?

Several more minutes passed quietly by, but she knew without looking up that he was still watching her. The question was, why?

When she couldn't stand it any longer she looked up and met his gaze. "Was there something you wanted?"

"No, ma'am," he said, his eyes never straying from her face. "Just enjoying the scenery."

Something in his eyes, in the intense way he stared, suggested that the scenery he was referring to was her. He was beginning to annoy the hell out of her, and she had the sinking feeling that was exactly his intention.

"Do you think you could possibly enjoy it from somewhere else?" she asked as politely as possible, despite her rapidly mounting irritation.

"What's wrong, Ivy?" He leaned forward on his elbows, deeper into her personal space. "Do I make you uncomfortable?"

That was the last thing she wanted him to think. He

no longer had *any* power over her. She was strong and independent. She answered to no one but herself. "No, but I would like to read a few more chapters before dinner. If you don't mind."

"Not at all. You go on ahead and read."

"Thank you." She turned her attention back to her book. He was quiet for several minutes, but in her peripheral vision she could see that he hadn't moved from his spot. He was still watching her.

He was definitely doing it to annoy her. There was no other logical explanation.

"I saw your mom a few weeks ago," he finally said.

She sighed and gathered her patience. So much for sitting outside, reading and enjoying the view.

She very calmly marked her page, shut the book and looked up at him. Ten years ago she would have thought he looked damned good standing there, the sun reflecting bluish-black off his dark hair, eyes slightly squinted against the glare and crinkled in the corners. The distinguished kind of crinkles that men got. The same things that on a woman were just plain old ugly wrinkles.

Dillon had that special something, a physical appeal that was impossible to ignore. Or resist. In the short term, anyway.

As she'd quickly discovered, looks aren't everything. What he needed was the personality to go along with it. One that wasn't quite so…*annoying*.

"You still fold your page over to mark your spot," he said. "No matter how many bookmarks you bought, you always misplaced them."

For a minute she was speechless. How had he remembered such a mundane, trivial detail about her? She honestly didn't think he'd been paying attention.

"Anyway," he continued, "I was in downtown Dallas for a meeting, and I saw your mom through the window of her shop. She looks as though she's doing well."

"She is." It had taken a while, but her mom had finally gotten her life together.

"I would have stopped in for a trim, but I was running late."

Only a complete fool would go to his former mother-in-law for a haircut. And while Dillon may have been a big pain in the behind, he was not a fool. Complete or otherwise.

"I figured I would stop in after my meeting instead. But then I got to thinkin', she may not have the highest opinion of me."

"Gosh, you think?" Her mom had *never* liked Dillon. Not even when they'd been dating. She'd always said he was too much like Ivy's real dad. Arrogant and unreliable.

After Ivy's dad took off, she and her mom had been forced to stay with Deidre and her parents until they got back on their feet.

He hadn't bothered to stick around, and her mom had been sure Dillon wouldn't, either. She'd warned Ivy repeatedly that she was asking for trouble, just begging to get her heart broken.

Ivy had wanted so badly to prove her wrong. But her mom had been right, of course, and to this day she'd never let Ivy live it down.

What would her mother think if she could see her

now, stuck in the same house with Dillon for a week? She would probably be worried that Ivy would be foolish enough to fall for him again. The way she had repeatedly fallen for Ivy's dad, trapped in what she liked to call an on-again, off-again trip through the house of horrors that had spanned nearly a decade.

Ivy was smarter than that. If there was one thing she'd learned from her mother, it was how not to repeat her mistakes.

She would worry about her mom Saturday when she flew in for the wedding. Right now she had other, more pressing problems, like the man still staring at her.

It was clear Dillon didn't intend to leave her alone. Rather than spend an hour or so before dinner enjoying the sun, she would instead have to remain indoors, where he couldn't bug her.

Ivy rose to her feet and grabbed her book. "I guess I'll see you at dinner."

"I thought you wanted to read."

"It's been a long day. I think I'll take a quick nap." It was a lie, but there was no way she would admit that he'd irritated her to the point of driving her away.

She hoped this was just his misguided way of trying to make amends. She hoped she was wrong and he wasn't actually doing this to annoy her.

"See ya'll later," he called, and as she was shutting the door, she could swear she heard laughter.

Three

Bitterness can be handled in many ways. The worst is to pretend it isn't there. Recognize it, identify it, embrace it. Then get over it.
—excerpt from *The Modern Woman's Guide to Divorce (And the Joy of Staying Single)*

Dillon was a big, fat liar.

Ivy sipped her champagne and glanced up at him through the pale pink, lingering light of sunset across the patio table. Eyes as blue and crisp as the ocean stared back, tangling her up in their gaze like a fish in a net.

A shivery zing of awareness started in her scalp and rippled with lightning speed down to her toes. And though she mentally squirmed and flopped, she couldn't seem to break loose.

Instead, she stared him down with a cool, disinterested look. Hoping he couldn't see the frantic flutter of her heartbeat at the base of her throat. The goose bumps dotting every conceivable inch of her flesh.

He was *supposed* to be avoiding her. He had *agreed* to leave her alone, hadn't he? Yet, as she feared earlier on the balcony, it was crystal clear that he had no intention of keeping his promise. In fact, he was doing everything he could to make her as uncomfortable as humanly possible.

And he did it damned well.

Throughout dinner, every time she looked up from her plate of mostly untouched food, his eyes were on her. He wasn't even attempting to be subtle, the big jerk.

At this rate she would be leaving the country a total basket case.

Blake kept shooting Ivy apologetic smiles, and Deidre had started stress eating. She had finished her own meal and was stealing bites from Blake's plate when she thought no one was watching. Blake's brothers, Calvin and Dale, observed with blatant curiosity.

Deidre's bridesmaids were another story. The motor-mouth twins—or as Deidre liked to call them, Tweedle Dee and Tweedle Dum—were too busy flapping their jaws to notice Ivy. Or anyone else for that matter.

They weren't actually twins, although they may as well have been. They had the same burnt-out blond hair and surgically enhanced, anorexic, size-one bodies. They even shared an identical flair for mindless, irrelevant conversation. Ivy was guessing that their collective IQ's ranked somewhere in the low double-digits.

"A toast to Deidre and Blake," Dillon said, raising his

glass, his eyes still locked on Ivy. She couldn't help but notice that he'd dropped the good ole boy twang. Tonight he sounded decidedly more upper-crust Dallas. "May you have a long, happy life together."

Like we didn't, his eyes seemed to say. Was he suggesting that was her fault?

Yeah, right.

Around the table crystal stemware clinked and everyone sipped. Ivy downed the contents of her glass in one long swallow. She'd never been much of a drinker, but the champagne felt good going down. It tickled her nose and warmed her nervous stomach.

One corner of Dillon's mouth tipped up and his eyes sparked with mischief. He was mocking her.

She sat a little straighter, pulled her shoulders back, all the more determined to see this through. She refused to let him win.

Maybe the trick to making it through this week was to drink alcohol. Lots and lots of alcohol. Hadn't that been Dillon's method of coping with stress? Hadn't he spent the better part of his time in college intoxicated?

Although she did notice that he drank only mineral water with dinner and had barely touched his champagne. Was it possible he'd given up drinking?

As if reading her thoughts, Dillon reached for the bottle of champagne the housekeeper had left chilling beside the table. He rose from his chair and circled to her side, moving with a subtle, yet undeniable male grace that was hypnotizing. Even the Tweedles, deep in some inane conversation about the difference between clothes sizes in the U.S. as opposed to Europe—in

Europe Dee had to buy a size three, *gasp!*—stopped to watch him with unguarded interest.

Ivy sat stock still, resisting the urge to turn in her chair as he stepped behind her. His aura seemed to suck the oxygen from the air around her, making her feel light-headed and woozy.

He leaned forward, resting a hand on the back of her chair—his fingers this close to her skin but not quite touching her—and filled her empty glass. As he poured, his arm brushed her shoulder.

His *bare* arm. Against her *bare* shoulder.

Time ground to a screeching halt, and the entire scene passed before her eyes in slow motion. A twisted, messy knot of emotions she couldn't even begin to untangle settled in her gut, and a weird, this-can't-possibly-be-happening feeling crept over her.

Why didn't she do something to stop him? Bat his hand away or jab an elbow into his gut? Why was she just sitting there frozen? It was not as if she was enjoying this.

Yet she couldn't deny that there was something about him, about the feel of his skin that was eerily familiar.

Not just familiar, but almost…natural. Which was just plain freaky, because there was nothing *natural* about her and Dillon being anywhere near each other.

Silence had fallen over the table and everyone stopped what they were doing to stare at her and Dillon.

Which Ivy realized was exactly what he wanted.

Under the table, her foot was tapping like mad. If she didn't calm down, she was going to wear away the sole of her sandal.

She forced herself to relax, to pretend she didn't care when in reality she was wound so tight she could crack walnuts on her rear end.

What felt like an eternity later he *finally* backed away, making it a point to run the length of his arm across her shoulder while the hand that rested behind her chair brushed ever so softly against the back of her neck. If this was what she had to look forward to every time she emptied her glass, maybe the heavy drinking wasn't such a hot idea after all. She was much better off keeping him at the opposite end of the table, where he could only touch her with his eyes.

"Anyone else?" he asked, offering a refill to the rest of the table.

Dee raised her glass. "I'd love some."

As he poured, Ivy couldn't help noticing that he didn't rest his hand on her chair, nor did he brush against her with his arm. Everyone else seemed to notice, too.

It confirmed that he had only been trying to antagonize her. Hadn't he caused her enough grief? Couldn't he act like an adult and leave her alone?

Just as she'd suspected. He hadn't changed a bit.

"Dale told us you guys used to be married," Dee said as Dillon returned to his side of the table and slid easily into his seat.

The way he could look so relaxed and casual, yet emanate an aura of authority, boggled the mind.

He retrieved his napkin from the table and draped it in his lap. "That's right."

Dee's eyes widened a fraction and she looked to Ivy for affirmation. "Really?"

"We were," Ivy confirmed. "For about a year. A long, *long* time ago."

"*He* married *you?*" Dum asked, looking first at Ivy, then to Dillon, shaking her head as if she couldn't believe what she was hearing. "Wow. I really thought Dale was kidding."

Gee, thanks, Ivy wanted to tell Miss Tactless. Just go ahead and say what's on your mind. Don't worry about my feelings.

"She left me and broke my heart," Dillon said, flashing Ivy a wry grin.

A look passed between the twins, like sharks who had just smelled blood in the water and were gearing up for a feast.

"*She* left *you?*" Dee, who obviously missed the sarcasm oozing from his words, clucked sympathetically, shooting Ivy a look of disdain. She reached across the table to pat Dillon's hand and assured him, "You deserve better."

Oh, please. Ivy experienced a severe mental eye roll. Even if she had wronged him somehow, which she absolutely hadn't, it had been ten years ago.

"It's no wonder," Dum said. "Blake, didn't you say she hates men?"

Deidre's jaw fell and she shot Blake a look.

"That's not what I said," Blake told her, shifting uncomfortably in his seat. He turned to Ivy, looking as though he wanted to disappear. "I swear, that's not what I said. I was just telling them about your book. Man-hating never entered the conversation."

Ivy believed him. In all the time she'd known Blake,

she'd never heard him say a disparaging word about anyone. But she could see the needle on Deidre's stress meter creeping into the red zone. Deidre eyed the Tweedles' untouched chocolate mousse with ravenous eyes and asked, "Would anyone like seconds on dessert?"

"Not me," Dillon said, rubbing a hand across what Ivy was sure was still a washboard stomach. "I'm stuffed."

"Like *she* needs seconds," Dee mumbled under her breath, but conveniently loud enough for the entire table to hear. Dum snickered and Blake's brothers exchanged a look, one that said Deidre's fluctuating weight had been a topic of conversation in the past.

That didn't surprise Ivy. The Tweedles hadn't exactly been Deidre's first choice for bridesmaids. In fact, they weren't her last choice, either. They ranked somewhere just below the never-in-a-million-years category. But Blake's brothers were the groomsmen, per their gazillionaire father's demands, and they had refused to stand up in the wedding without their girlfriends.

Since Deidre would be stuck as a part of the family for the next fifty years or so, and Daddy was footing the bill for the wedding—and the house they were moving into after the honeymoon, *and* the cars they would be driving—Deidre felt it best to acquiesce.

The whole arrangement set off warning bells for Ivy, but she was keeping her mouth shut. Deidre seemed happy, and Ivy didn't want to burst her bubble. There was a very slim chance it would all work out, and Ivy was clinging to that hope.

An uncomfortable silence fell over the table, and Deidre lowered her eyes to her lap, shame flaring in red-hot splotches across her cheeks. Blake looked awkwardly around, everywhere but at the woman he should have been speaking up to defend. Ivy felt torn between defending her cousin and not wanting to make things worse.

Blake was a genuinely nice guy, and he loved Deidre. Unfortunately, he didn't have much in the way of a backbone.

Of the three brothers he was the youngest, and while he hadn't taken a beating with the ugly stick, he wasn't what you would call a looker, either. He was sort of…nondescript, and he let everyone, including his family—*especially his family*—walk all over him.

Which is why Ivy feared Deidre would be bowing to her in-laws' wishes for the rest of her natural life.

"So, Ivy, I hear you're a practicing psychologist now," Dillon said.

Uh-oh. She distinctly felt an attack coming on.

Wonderful.

At the very least, taking potshots at her would deflect the attention from Deidre. It would be worth a little humiliation.

"Yes, I am," Ivy said, unable to keep the defensive lilt from her voice. One corner of Dillon's mouth quirked up in a very subtle grin, and Ivy raised her chin, bracing for the onslaught of insults. The "shrink" jokes she'd already heard a million times. The "little book" jabs.

She fisted her hands in her lap, digging her nails in the heels of her palms, her foot tapping like mad under the table, steeling herself for the worst.

Bring it on, pal.

"I find it truly fascinating," Dillon said, and Ivy thought, *sure you do.*

Dee covered a yawn with fingers tipped in bright pink, clawlike nails, and Dum made a production of looking at her watch. Did they think they were the queens of stimulating conversation?

Dale and Calvin, on the other hand, looked thoroughly amused by the entire situation. Those two were even worse than Dillon. They needed to grow up and get a life.

"Her book has been on the *New York Times* bestseller list for months," Deidre said, a note of pride in her voice. "She's famous."

Unimpressed, the Tweedles rolled their eyes.

"I'm particularly interested in the study of self-esteem," Dillon said.

Self-esteem?

Was that some sort of veiled insult? Was he honestly suggesting that Ivy had low self-esteem?

She felt her blood pressure shoot up to a dangerously high level, and her foot was cramping up from the workout it was getting.

She was incredibly comfortable with herself, *thank you very much.*

"I once read that people with a negative or low self-esteem will insult and belittle other people to boost their own egos." His expression was serious, but there was a spark of pure mischief in Dillon's eyes. His gaze strayed briefly to the Tweedles, then back to Ivy. "Is that true?"

It took a full ten seconds for the impact of his words to settle in, and when it did, Ivy was so surprised she nearly laughed out loud.

He *wasn't* attacking her. His observations were aimed directly at the twins.

"That is true," she told him, in her therapist's, I'm-not-speaking-of-anyone-in-particular-just-stating-the-scientific-evidence tone.

Dale and Calvin weren't looking so cocky now, and a grateful smile had begun to creep over Deidre's face.

The Tweedles were a bit slower to catch on.

Ivy watched with guilty pleasure as the two of them digested his words with brains no doubt impaired by bleach overexposure. She relished the look of stunned indignation on their faces when the meaning hit home.

She had never been an advocate of "an eye for an eye" and preferred not to lower herself to the Tweedles' level, but it felt damned good to knock those two down a peg.

"In fact," she continued, "self-esteem is one of the most widely studied areas of psychology."

"Why is that?" Dillon asked, feeding the flames, while the Tweedles grew increasingly uncomfortable.

Her conscience told her that what she was about to do was childish and just plain mean, but she couldn't deny the satisfaction she felt watching the Tweedles squirm. And who knows, maybe her words would strike some sort of chord, and they would think of other people's feelings for a change.

Should she or shouldn't she?

Oh, what the hell.

"Because self-esteem plays a role in virtually everything we do," she explained. "A lack of it can have dire effects. People who are unsure of themselves sometimes have trouble sustaining healthy relationships.

Since they often feel embarrassed and ashamed without due cause, their irrational reactions tend to baffle and alienate others."

"That *is* fascinating," Deidre agreed, casting a grin Ivy's way.

On a roll now, Ivy added, "Even worse, low self-esteem can cause or contribute to neurosis, anxiety, defensiveness, eating disorders and even alcohol and drug abuse."

"How tragic," Dillon said, looking pointedly to Blake's brothers. "Don't you think?"

Dale and Calvin exchanged an uneasy look, but neither uttered a sound. It was clear they were of the collective opinion that they shouldn't mess with the billionaire oil man.

The balance of power had just been established. At least for once Dillon had used that clout and influence for someone's benefit other than his own.

She would have to thank him later.

"Well, I think I'll take a walk on the beach before it gets dark," Dillon said, rising to his feet, and with his eyes on Ivy asked, "Anyone care to join me?"

As if. She wasn't *that* grateful.

"I will!" Deidre said, popping up from her chair with such enthusiasm that she bumped the table and sent her champagne glass teetering precariously. Blake grabbed it before it could topple over and shatter against the glass-top table. It was a nice save and, if Deidre's doe-eyed smile was any indication, might just compensate for his letting her down earlier.

Blake stood, brushing remnants of his dinner from the front of his clothes. Clothes that hung on his narrow, gangly frame. No matter how well he dressed, he always looked a tad…untidy. "I'll come, too."

"We're going into town to hit the bars," Dale said, answering for that side of the table. All four of them looked as though they could use a stiff drink. Or maybe five. Hopefully, in the future they would take the time to think about what they were saying before they opened their mouths, and realize there were certain people you just didn't mess with. Not without getting burned.

Ivy rose from her chair. "I'm going to head up to my room. I have to check my e-mail."

"But you promised no work this week," Deidre said with a pout.

"I know, but I'm expecting a message from my editor," she lied. The truth was, she'd told her editor, agent and writing partner that this week had been reserved strictly for relaxation.

What a joke. There would be nothing relaxing about this week. She would be lucky if she didn't return to Texas a certified Froot Loop in need of intensive psychotherapy.

Deidre clutched Ivy's hand in a death grip. "Come with us. *Please.*"

Ivy knew what she was trying to do, and it wasn't going to work. She wanted Ivy to forgive Dillon. To "get past it," whatever "it" was.

Yes, Dillon had done something nice, shown that he had an unselfish side, but it didn't excuse the way he'd taunted her all evening. It also didn't change the fact that he would most likely continue to taunt and harass her until she boarded the plane Sunday morning.

She pried her hand free. "Next time. I promise."

Deidre looked as if she wanted to press the issue but let it drop.

Everyone went their separate ways, and Ivy headed upstairs, feeling uneasy and not quite sure why. Something weird had just happened down there. Something disturbing that she couldn't quite put her finger on.

She stepped into her room, closed the door and leaned against it.

A disaster had been diverted, thanks to Dillon. She would go so far as to say the entire situation, while childish and petty, had actually been fun—

Wait a minute. *Fun?* With *Dillon?*

The truth grabbed hold and shook her silly for a second.

That's what was so weird. Tonight had reminded her, if only for a few seconds, that at one time she and Dillon had made a good team. They used to have fun.

Even worse, she was pretty sure she actually disliked him a little less than she had this morning.

Oh, this was bad.

Hating Dillon was her only defense, her only ammunition. She depended on it.

Without that hate, she could no longer ignore the fact that he'd irreparably broken her heart.

Four

Do you suspect your man is lying to you? Trust your intuition. Odds are, he probably is.
—excerpt from *The Modern Woman's Guide to Divorce (And the Joy of Staying Single)*

Ivy learned two important lessons that night.

The first was that the only thing worse than having to face her ex again was having to face him in her ratty old nightshirt with the sleeves torn off, wet, tangled hair and no makeup.

The second, more valuable, lesson was always lock your bedroom door.

"Whoops," Dillon said from the open doorway when he saw her lying in bed on her stomach, on top of the covers, her laptop open in front of her.

She scrambled onto her knees, tugging the shirt down over her pale, sun-deprived legs, kicking herself for not visiting the tanning bed a few times before she left. Then kicking herself a second time for caring what he thought. "What are you doing in here?"

He looked genuinely baffled. "Guess I got the wrong room."

She couldn't help wondering how he'd managed that, since Deidre had had the decency not to put them in adjacent rooms and his was located at the opposite end of the house.

"Huh." Dillon glanced down the hall in the direction he'd come from. "I must'a made a wrong turn at the stairs."

She dragged her fingers through her knotted hair, cursing herself for not running a brush through it. Her mother, the cosmetologist, had spent years hammering into her head that to avoid damage to the ends and give her thin hair more body, it should be brushed *after* it dried. Which shouldn't have been a problem since she hadn't been anticipating company.

Or in Dillon's case, an intruder.

You don't care, she reminded herself.

"Well, as you can see, this isn't your room, so…good night."

He looked casually around, as if he had every right to be there. "Hey, this is nice."

"Yeah, it's great." And she knew for a fact it was not much different than his room.

Rather than leave, Dillon stepped farther inside, wedging his hands in the front pockets of his jeans. A move completely nonthreatening, but she felt herself tense. "I think your room is bigger than mine. And damn, look at that view."

Without invitation, and in a move arrogantly typical of him, he crossed the room to the open French doors and stepped outside onto the balcony.

Ugh! The man was insufferable!

Forgetting about her unsightly white skin, she jumped up out of bed and followed him. Staring at her from a balcony a dozen yards away was one thing. She could even live with the teasing, but this was her room, her only refuge this week, and he had no right to just barge in uninvited. "What do you think you're doing?"

The sun had dipped below the horizon, leaving only a hazy magenta ghost in its wake, and specks of glittering light dotted the heavens. And in the not so far distance she could hear the waves crashing against the bluff. Add to that the cool breeze blowing off the water and it was a perfect night. If not for the man standing there.

He whistled low and shook his head. "Yes, ma'am, quite a view."

"Your room faces the same ocean, so I doubt the view is all that different at the opposite end of the house. Hey, I have an idea. Why don't you go check."

Ignoring the razor-sharp edge of irritation in her voice, he propped both hands on the railing and made himself comfortable. "No, sir, you don't see stars like this in Dallas." He sucked in a long, deep breath and blew it out. "No smog, either."

She wasn't quite sure of the point of the "aw, shucks"

routine, but it was getting really annoying. "Dillon, I want you to leave."

He turned to her, his face partially doused in shadow, wearing that crooked grin. "No, you don't."

Damn him. He still knew exactly which buttons to push. But she wasn't going to take the bait. She wasn't the young, emotionally adolescent girl he remembered. She was going to stay calm. "Yes, *I do*."

"It's been ten years. We have a lot of catching up to do." His eyes strayed to the front of the threadbare, oversize shirt and the grin went from amused to carnal.

Exactly what kind of catching up did he think they would be doing? And was he familiar with the phrase, *when hell freezes over?*

"You always did wear T-shirts to bed. Usually mine." He hooked his thumbs in the front pockets of his jeans and something dangerously hot flickered in his eyes. "You said you liked 'em 'cause they smelled like me."

She crossed her arms and shot him a chilling look.

Undaunted, his eyes wandered over her. "And I see that you still wait until your hair is dry to brush it."

She hated that he still knew her so well. That he'd bothered to remember anything about her at all. And the only reason he had was to use it against her. To make her uncomfortable. To knock her off balance and lower her defenses so he could go in for the kill.

She wouldn't give him the satisfaction.

"I'll bet you do all those things subconsciously," he mused. "Because deep down you still love me and you want me back."

The mercury on her temper began a steady climb, and

she clamped her teeth over the sarcastic reply that was trying like hell to jump out of her mouth.

You will not show this man how angry he's making you, she chanted to herself. *You will not let him get the best of you.*

"Isn't there a technical term for that?" he asked.

Yeah, there was a term for it.

Nuts.

Which he was if he honestly believed she had any feelings left for him. Favorable ones, that is.

"Don't we have a high opinion of ourselves," she said.

He grinned. "Maybe, but you can't say that I'm not consistent."

No, she definitely couldn't say that. He'd never once failed to let her down.

And this conversation was going nowhere.

"Look, I appreciate the way you defended Deidre against the Tweedles at dinner, but let's not pretend that I don't know exactly what you're doing and why you're doing it."

Amusement quirked up the corner of his mouth. "Tweedles?"

Ivy slapped a hand over her mouth. Oh, jeez. Had she really said that out loud?

"Like Tweedle Dee and Tweedle Dum?" A deep rumble of infectious laughter rolled from his chest and had a grin tugging at the corners of her own mouth.

And just as quickly it fizzled away.

Ugh!

He was doing it again. Softening her up. Lowering the ick factor of just being near him.

"You need to leave," she said. "I have work to finish."

He didn't move. "I guess you got that e-mail from your editor, huh?"

"That's right," she fibbed. "I'm incredibly busy right now."

"Why don't I believe you?" He eased away from the ledge, and she resisted the urge to step back. "You know, I could always tell when you were lying."

"I guess it takes one to know one," she snapped.

The humor slipped from his face, and she could see that she'd hit a nerve. Well, good. He had it coming.

Then why did she feel like such a louse?

He took another step closer. "Did I ever lie to you, Ivy?"

"I am not doing this." She turned and walked to the closet. She flung the door open and snatched her robe from the hanger. "I refuse to get sucked into a conversation about a relationship that has been over for ten years."

She thrust her arms through the sleeves and bound the belt securely at her waist. She swung around and nearly plowed into him. He was right behind her.

"The truth, Ivy." Every trace of playful cockiness had disappeared from his voice. "Did I ever once lie to you?"

Her heart rattled around in her chest. She remembered this man. The quiet, serious, alter ego. His appearances had been rare, but they had always intimidated the hell out of her. And Dillon knew it.

Had he been hiding in the background all this time, waiting for just the right moment to pounce?

"I don't owe you a thing."

He stepped closer, his eyes locked on her face, and

every cell in her body went on full alert, every neuron in her brain lit off like fireworks on the Fourth of July.

"Did I *ever* lie to you?"

Don't do it, she warned her traitorous subconscious. Don't you dare say what you're thinking. It doesn't matter anymore. It will only make things worse.

Don't say a word.

He stepped closer, until he was only inches away. His hair was a little windblown from his walk along the beach, and she could smell the scent of the ocean on his skin and clothes. Steel-blue eyes bore through her, stripping her bare, and her feet felt cemented to the floor.

She couldn't move.

"Ivy?"

"No!" she shrieked, no longer able to contain the anger and frustration and hurt that had been festering for far too long. "You never lied to me, Dillon. In fact, you made it distinctly clear just how little our marriage meant to you."

She regretted the words the instant they left her mouth, but it was too late to take them back. She was still bitter and hurt by the divorce and now he knew it. And she didn't doubt he would use it against her.

For several long seconds he just stared at her, his expression impossible to decipher. Finally, his voice neither warm nor cold, he said, "I wasn't the one who walked out the door."

His words felt like a slap across the face and literally knocked her back a step. He wasn't suggesting the demise of their marriage was *her* fault, was he? There was only one person to blame, and he was standing right in front of her.

Who had repeatedly stayed out every night and come home drunk while she had done her best to get an education? Who had blown his money gambling week after week?

And who had sicced his father on the grant committee and had her scholarship revoked?

Maybe he hadn't lied, but what he'd done was worse. He'd let her down.

For a second they just stood there looking at each other, then he shook his head, so subtly she had to wonder if she'd really seen it or if it had been a trick of the light.

"Good night, Ivy." He turned and left, closing the door quietly behind him.

And for some stupid reason she felt like crying.

She didn't care what he believed. What had happened to their marriage was not her fault. She may have been the one to physically walk out the door, but emotionally, Dillon had already been long gone.

Ivy dove into the pool, limbs slicing across the still water like a hot knife through cool butter. Thanks to Mr. I-never-lied-to-you, she'd slept like hell and woke at dawn. But with each stroke she could feel the stress from the previous night begin to evaporate, burned away by the adrenaline and endorphins coursing through her bloodstream.

She'd always had something of a love/hate relationship with exercise. She'd been blessed with a naturally slim figure, so her sporadic visits to the gym never caused her concern. In the last few years, however, she'd noticed things gradually beginning to expand and spread.

Hence her daily morning swim. It was the one thing that felt the least like real exercise. And while it wouldn't bring back the figure of her youth, she was able to comfortably maintain her present weight.

She only wished some of that extra weight had been redistributed to her less than impressive bustline.

She completed her laps and surfaced, and there, not three feet away, lay Dillon in a lounge chair beside the pool, a mug of coffee in one hand. Watching her, of course.

Here we go again.

She couldn't see what he had on from the waist down, other than the fact that his feet and calves were bare, but from the waist up he wore a deep tan and a sleepy smile. One that said, *hmm, how can I mess with Ivy today?*

She ignored the sudden lightness in her chest, the jittery, nervous feeling in her stomach. She repressed the *why me* groan working its way up her chest.

"Morning," he said. Dark stubble shadowed his jaw and his hair had that mussed, just-rolled-out-of-the-sack look.

She wondered how long he'd been sitting there watching her. She'd never seen him crawl out of bed before ten in the morning. Usually it was closer to noon.

She swam to the ladder and climbed out, facing away from him, feeling uncomfortable despite her modest one-piece suit. It was still too revealing. Too likely to show off the changes in her body, when his own physique appeared to have only improved with age.

And really, why did she care?

She wrapped herself in a towel, squeezing the excess water from her hair. "You're awake early."

"I'm an early riser these days."

Just her luck. More time he could spend harassing her.

Yet nothing good would come of letting him see that he was irritating her. Last night was an unfortunate setback. It was imperative that today she play it cool. She had to be patient.

She grabbed her iced coffee from the table where she'd left it and turned to her ex. When she realized how he was dressed, the cup nearly slipped from her grasp.

Deep down in the rational part of her brain, she knew he was going for shock value. She knew the appropriate reaction was no reaction at all.

Unfortunately, at the moment, her rational brain was not calling the shots. *"What are you wearing?"*

He looked down to his lap, at what appeared to be a pair of very expensive black silk boxers. "Skivvies," he said casually, as though there was nothing at all inappropriate about walking around a strange house in his underwear. "I would have put on pajamas, but as I'm sure you recall, I don't wear any. Besides," he said, with a slight wiggle of his eyebrows, "it's nothing you haven't seen before."

"There are six other people in this house, you know."

"And they're all sound asleep."

"Not to mention the housekeep—" She stopped abruptly and spun away from him. "For pity's sake, at least have the decency to button your fly."

"Whoops," she heard him say, although he didn't sound all that concerned with his faux pas. The man would go to any lengths to make her uncomfortable. "No wonder the housekeeper looked at me funny when I was pouring my coffee." There was a short pause, then he said, "The stallion is locked back in the stable. You can turn around now."

Facing him meant he would possibly see the red patches of embarrassment blooming across her cheeks. But not facing him would be even worse.

She turned, keeping her eyes above neck level. Looking at his bare chest reminded her of touching his bare chest, which reminded her of other things they used to do. Which would only make the blush burn brighter.

"When did you start swimming?" he asked. "I seemed to recall you hating exercise."

"I still do, but some of us have to work at it."

"And you're assumin' I don't? Would it surprise you to learn that I go to the gym every morning before work?"

Being surprised wasn't the issue. She didn't want to know about his life. It humanized him, made him seem like a regular guy. She preferred to keep him in the niche she'd carved out for him. That place in her mind where he would always be arrogant and cocky and totally unappealing.

"Although I never did learn how to swim," he said, which she found incredibly hard to swallow. True, she'd never actually seen him swim, but his home had been highlighted on some decorating show on cable television—or so someone had told her. From what she heard he owned a big, fancy mansion—she might have even driven past it one time, accidentally, of course—where he'd installed an Olympic-size indoor pool. He wasn't married, didn't have children. Why install a pool if he didn't plan to use it?

"You should try it sometime," she said.

"Are you going golfing today?" he asked, referring to the golf outing Blake and Deidre had scheduled.

Apparently, he didn't remember everything about her. She did not golf.

She was about to tell him no, she didn't plan to go, but caught herself. There was only one thing Dillon had loved more than drinking and gambling. That was golfing. But if he knew she wasn't going, he might very well skip it and spend the entire day harassing her.

"I'm going," she lied.

"Blake said we're meeting in the foyer at ten-fifteen."

That could be a problem. If she didn't show, he would know she wasn't going. Of course, if she was already gone by ten-fifteen, he would have no idea where to look for her. It shouldn't be all that tough to slip away. "Well then, I should hurry back to my room and get ready."

"Wear something cool," he called after her as she rushed inside. "It's going to be a scorcher."

"Will do!" she shot back. She could sneak out of the house by ten, and Dillon would never be the wiser. And she would have the entire day all to herself.

Five

Is your ex harassing you? Trying to intimidate you? Take action and beat him at his own game! It's easier than you may think.
—excerpt from *The Modern Woman's Guide to Divorce (And the Joy of Staying Single)*

He'd reduced himself to stalking.

Dillon followed several yards behind Ivy as she browsed the merchandise lining the streets of the shopping district. He'd been following her since she snuck out of the house this morning.

He couldn't help thinking that he'd sunk pitifully low, but he had to keep his eye on the prize. Seeing Ivy broken and begging for forgiveness.

The sun brought out the reddish-gold highlights in

her hair, and a cool breeze blowing off the ocean ruffled the full, filmy-looking skirt she wore, playing a tantalizing game of peek-a-boo with those long, toned, milky-white legs.

She wore a simple, pale blue tank top that settled nicely on shoulders that, on someone else, would have been too narrow and angular. But everything about her body fit just right. He wasn't the only one who noticed, either. As she wandered down the cobblestone street, dignified and maybe a touch aloof, heads turned and eyes looked on with interest.

But he knew something they didn't. He knew the feisty, passionate girl she hid behind that curtain of quiet grace. There were times when he missed that woman. But she had disappeared the moment they'd said *I do.*

He wondered what it would take to draw her out. If she even existed any longer. Somehow he doubted it.

It might be fun finding out though.

Ivy picked up a bottle of something from a table, perfume maybe, and lifted it to her nose. She closed her eyes and inhaled deeply, a dreamy look on her face.

The vendor behind the table said something, and she smiled and shook her head. A genuine, easy smile. One he hadn't seen in a very long time. Even on the inside jacket of her book, which he had grudgingly skimmed at Barnes & Noble, she'd been all business. And near the end of their marriage neither had done much in the way of smiling. Not at each other, anyway.

That had always been Ivy's problem. She was too repressed and too driven. She'd never learned how to have fun. At least, not out of the bedroom. And it wasn't as if he hadn't tried to teach her. They had been making good progress, then they got married and she did a one-eighty on him.

After a bit of haggling, she reached into the pack she wore around her waist, pulled out several bills and handed them to the vendor. She slipped her purchase inside her pack and moved on to the next canopy.

She looked so relaxed and serene. At peace with herself and the world.

A grin curled his mouth. What better time to mosey up and say hello?

"Well, well, what a coincidence," he drawled from behind her in that counterfeit twang he knew grated on her nerves.

Her hand stilled midair, just short of the colorful silk shawl she'd been about to look at, and every inch of her went rigid.

This was too easy. Better than greeting her this morning in his underwear, although that had been pretty damned funny. She obviously hadn't noticed the robe draped over the chair beside him.

Still only seeing what she wanted to see, believing what she wanted to believe.

Ivy paused and took a deep breath, as if gathering her strength—or maybe her patience—then turned to face him. She'd sufficiently wiped any trace of emotion from her face, but she forgot who she was dealing with. He picked up on the subtle signs no one else noticed. The crinkle in her brow and the slight tightening of her jaw. The way she ground her teeth and narrowed her eyes the tiniest bit.

Things she probably wasn't even aware she was doing.

She could pretend she wasn't annoyed, but he knew better.

"Why do I sincerely doubt this is a coincidence?" she asked.

He shrugged. "It wouldn't have anything to do with you bein' somethin' of a pessimist, now would it?"

"What are you doing here?"

He flashed her a grin and held up the bag he was carrying. "Souvenirs. For my secretary."

"Lingerie?" she guessed.

"Nah. My preferences in sleepwear lean toward the casual. Oversize T-shirts…" He leaned closer, lowering his voice. "Or nothing at all."

She rolled her eyes.

"Not to mention the fact that my secretary is sixty-eight."

"Aren't you supposed to be playing golf?"

"Shopping sounded like more fun."

She let an undignified snort slip out. "Now I *know* you're lying. You love playing golf, and you always hated shopping."

"That is true. It's the company I wasn't all that thrilled about. What was it you called them? The Tweedles?"

It wasn't a lie. He'd had more of those two than he could stomach at dinner last night. And torturing Ivy won out over golf any day of the week. He just had to accidentally bump into her, the way he'd "accidentally" walked into her room. What he hadn't counted on last night was getting himself sucked into a touchy-feely debate about their failed marriage.

She was still trying to pin the blame on him. No big surprise there.

Miss Perfect. Miss Nothing-is-ever-good-enough-for-me. Maybe he'd made a mistake or two, *minor ones,* but if anyone was ultimately responsible for the divorce, it was her.

And why had she assumed that what he'd done at dinner last night had anything to do with her? He was merely helping a friend. Blake was a good guy, the kind who would give a stranger the shirt off his back in the middle of a blizzard. But as long as Dillon had known him, Blake let his family walk all over him. With golf cleats on.

Deidre was the perfect match for him. Soft-spoken and demure, and maybe a little awkward. Although Dillon sensed there was more to her than met the eye, the spark of something more complex. A confidence that she hadn't let herself explore. If that was the case, Dillon suspected that she would only take so much more from his family before she blew a gasket.

He hoped so. Otherwise, they would eat her for breakfast.

"Well," Ivy said with a forced smile. "It was…nice seeing you again."

He chuckled. "Now, that's a lie if I ever heard one."

"You're right, it is a lie. Goodbye." She turned and marched off, weaving her way through the crowd of people clogging the streets. Did she really think he was going to let her off that easy?

This was a vacation, and he intended to have fun.

* * *

Ivy zigzagged her way through the crowd, resisting the urge to break into a run and let Dillon see her desperation.

The market was hot and noisy, the air filled with the spicy scent of unfamiliar and delectable foods she had been hoping to sample. There were a million different things to see and do, places to explore.

And she'd planned to do it alone.

Barely thirty seconds passed before she heard Dillon say, "Where's the fire?"

She groaned to herself. He wasn't going to leave her alone. He was going to dog her all afternoon, like a joy-sucking leech. And how had he managed to find her? She'd waited until no one was around to sneak out of the house, and she hadn't told anyone, not even Deidre, where she was going.

Had he lied about golf? Had he hidden somewhere and waited for her to leave, then followed her? Would he be that devious?

Dumb question. Of course he would.

What had she done to deserve this?

She could play this two ways. She could act as though she didn't care, or she could bluntly tell him to leave her the hell alone. But she knew Dillon. Admitting he was annoying her would only fuel his determination. The best way to possibly get rid of him, the *only* way, was to pretend she didn't care either way. Eventually he would get bored and find someone else to torture. She hoped.

Either way she would be stuck with him for the rest of the afternoon. Maybe longer.

Yahoo. She could hardly wait.

She cast him a sideways glance. He walked beside her, thumbs hooked loosely in the front pockets of his jeans, casual as you please, and for an instant she felt a tiny bit breathless. He wore a pair of faded Levi's, polished cowboy boots and a white tank top that accentuated the golden tan of his shoulders, the lean definition in his biceps. His hair had that casual, slightly mussed look, as if he'd just rolled out of bed and run his fingers through it. Which is what he used to do ten years ago.

But when a person looked at him, really looked, it was clear there was more to him than just a pretty face. You could see the breeding, the auspicious roots.

He wore his status well. It complemented, but didn't define him.

"So, you're a hotshot author now," he said.

"If you say so." She tried to keep it light and brief. She didn't want to say the wrong thing and give him a new round of ammunition to fire her way.

"I heard you're writing a followup to that little book of yours."

"Did you?" He could condescend all he liked, but that "little" book had made more money than she and the co-author, Miranda Reed, had ever imagined possible.

Having both endured grueling, nasty divorces, the project had been more therapeutic than financially motivated. They hadn't even been sure anyone would want to publish it. In fact, they had been fairly certain the manuscript would sit untouched on some apathetic editor's desk, yellowing at the edges and gathering dust.

Not only did it sell, it became ensnared in a bidding

war between several publishing houses. Since its release it had been topping the bestseller lists. It was a pure fluke that it had struck a chord with so many readers. And disturbing to discover the staggering number of women who had endured, or were presently experiencing, painful divorces.

It had solidified Ivy's belief that happy, successful marriages were a rare anomaly not experienced by the majority of the population. And with very few exceptions, women were better off staying single.

"I would think you'd have run out of material by now," Dillon said.

Was the hotshot billionaire afraid he would be seeing his checkered past in print again?

Well, well. This was interesting.

"Do I detect a note of concern?" she asked.

"The truth is, I was thinkin' maybe I'll write a book, too."

If he was trying to scare her, he would have to do better. "Good luck with that."

"A tell-all with every intimate detail of our marriage." He grinned and nodded his head, as if he was really warming to the idea. "Yeah. Or better yet, maybe I should send a letter or two to *Penthouse Forum*."

"Sex with you was not that exciting," she said, knowing as well as he did that it was a big fat lie. Near the end, their sex life had been as volatile as their tempers, as if they had been taking out all their frustrations in bed.

"Are you forgetting the time we got creative with that bottle of hot fudge and you let me lick it off your—"

"I remember," she interjected, fighting the blush that

had begun to creep up from her collar. Hot fudge hadn't been the only food they'd experimented with. She had fond memories of a can of whipped cream and a bottle of maraschino cherries.

"And if memory serves, you had a particularly sensitive spot, right here…" He reached up and brushed the tip of his index finger against the spot just below her ear.

She instinctively batted his hand away, but not before a ripple of erotic sensation whispered across her skin, making her feel warm and shivery at the same time. She shot him a warning look.

His victory triggered a triumphant, smug grin. "Yes, ma'am, it's still there."

"Try it again and you'll lose that finger." Verbal torment was one thing. Touching was off limits.

"I think I just figured out your problem."

So had she. He was walking right beside her.

But she had to ask, "Which problem would that be?"

"Sex."

Sex? Oh, she couldn't wait to see where he was going with this. "My problem is sex?"

"I'll bet you haven't had it in a long time."

She thought back to Deidre's comment about Ivy's less than active sex life. The truth was, she hadn't been with a man, hadn't had time for a relationship, much less a one-night stand, in so long she wasn't sure she remembered how. But as she told Deidre, she didn't need a man to complete her. And if she was looking for sexual release, she didn't need a man for that, either.

"And you're basing this assumption on what exactly?" she asked Dillon.

"Though you try to repress it, you're a very passionate person. Passionate people need sex regularly or they get cranky. And darlin', you are about as cranky as they come."

Did it ever occur to him that *he* was the one making her cranky?

"It can't be just any sex, either," he went on. "It has to be damned good, preferably with someone who knows exactly what it takes to light their fire."

And she was pretty sure he was offering to do the job. Did he honestly think he could charm his way back into her bed? Could he possibly be that arrogant?

Of course he could.

The real question was, what did she plan to do about it? How would she put him in his place and teach him a lesson he should have learned a long time ago?

She would do the one thing he would never expect. The only thing that would knock *him* completely off balance.

She stopped abruptly, right in the middle of the street, in front of God and everyone, and turned to face him. Before he could get his bearings, or she had a second of clarity to talk herself out of it, she reached up and curled her fingers into the front of his shirt. She wrapped her other hand around the back of his neck and tugged him down to her level.

He smelled of soap and shampoo and his hair was soft around her fingers. His wide-eyed surprise was the last thing she saw as she planted a kiss right on his damp and slightly parted lips.

* * *

Just when Dillon thought he had Ivy pegged, she did something completely off the wall and totally out of character. He'd expected some sort of reaction from her. One of those cool, deadly stares or a snippy remark. The last thing he'd expected was a kiss.

And he sure as hell hadn't expected to enjoy it.

One brush of her full, soft lips, one taste of her sweet mouth, and the memory of the fighting, the bitter, angry words they had flung at each other like daggers, misted like the ocean spray, then evaporated in the hot, dry Mexican air.

It came on swift and sudden, like a sniper attack, and before his brain had a chance to catch up with his body to process the acute physical response, it was over.

In a flash he was back on the noisy, crowded street. Ivy stood with her hands propped on her hips, looking up at him. Her eyes cold. In that instant he understood exactly what she was doing and what she meant to accomplish. And for reasons he didn't understand—or didn't want to admit—he felt cheated.

No one had looked at him with the same genuine and honest admiration as Ivy had. As long as he could remember, his family name had afforded him certain privileges. With little more than a snap of his fingers he could have had any woman he desired.

Ivy had been the only one he'd ever *needed*.

She saw through him, to the real man inside. She understood him in a way no one else had. Or maybe she had been the only one who bothered to try.

She studied him for a good thirty seconds, looking almost bored, then shrugged. "Nothing."

Ouch. She'd scored one on him, no doubt, and it had been a direct hit.

"I guess you just don't do it for me anymore," she said apologetically. "But I appreciate the offer."

She spun away, skirt swishing around her legs. Only then did it register; the slight tremble in her voice, her pulse throbbing at the base of her throat and the smudge of color riding the arch of her cheeks.

A man didn't spend a year of marriage without learning a woman's signals. And he could read hers loud and clear. He wasn't the only one turned on by that kiss. She wanted him, too.

This called for a slight change of plans. There was only one thing that could possibly be more fun than annoying Ivy, and that would be getting back into her panties. That would be the ultimate payback.

He was smiling as he set off after her. It looked as if they would be taking this competition to an all new level.

Six

*Divorce recovery typically takes two full years.
Take it day by day. Trust me, the time will soon
come when you'll look back and wonder what you
ever saw in him.*
—excerpt from *The Modern Woman's Guide to
Divorce (And the Joy of Staying Single)*

Kiss your ex-husband. Brilliant idea.

As fast as her wobbly legs would carry her, Ivy
headed blindly in what she hoped was the general direction of the villa, praying that Dillon didn't follow her.

Weathered stucco buildings, brightly colored can-
opies and an ocean of moving bodies blurred together
like smudged oil paint on a three-dimensional canvas.
Voices and sounds echoed through her ears and jumbled

around inside her head, disorienting her. Her hands were trembling and her heart beat hard and fast in her chest.

One stupid kiss and she was a walking disaster area. *What had she been thinking?*

It wasn't supposed to happen this way. She was supposed to be proving how over him she was. She wasn't supposed to *enjoy* kissing him.

She wasn't supposed to *feel* anything.

And if she had to feel something, why couldn't it have been hate? Disgust would have been a good one, too. Or good old-fashioned anger.

And what if by some remote chance someone recognized them? Someone who had read her book? What if word got out that she was messing around with her ex? What would people think of her? How could her readers, not to mention her patients, trust her if she couldn't even follow her own edict?

This was bad.

Really, *really* bad.

Although she had to admit that seeing the stunned look on his face, knowing that for once *she* had flustered *him,* had almost been worth it. In a sadistic sort of way. Like cutting off her nose to spite her face.

"You sure move fast when you have something to run from," Dillon said from behind her, and Ivy cursed under her breath.

Oh, crud.

She needed a minute to pull herself together. She couldn't let him see her thrown so far off-kilter.

This was just a fluke. She'd been too immersed in her

career, too swamped promoting her first book and writing the second to even think about sex, so, yeah, she'd overreacted a little.

Okay, she'd overreacted *a lot*. But she would have gotten the same result from kissing any number of men.

She tried to conjure up a name, an appealing, eligible man in her life. Maybe one in the office building where she worked, or at the club where she used the pool. Or even at the grocery store. There had to be *someone*.

Yet not a single one came to mind.

Oh, hell, who was she kidding? She could continue to blame her busy schedule, but deep down she knew that was bunk. The reason she hadn't slept with anyone in…well, longer than she wanted to admit, was because she hadn't met anyone she wanted to sleep with. Up until today.

Oh, no. She did *not* just think that. She didn't want to sleep with Dillon. Not now, not ever.

"And what is it exactly that I'm running from?" she asked. She even managed to keep her voice steady and vaguely disinterested.

The deep baritone of laughter that followed rubbed across every one of her nerve endings until they felt raw and exposed.

He knew. He knew exactly what that kiss had done to her, and he would spend the rest of the week rubbing it in her face.

Would this nightmare never end?

She was about to turn, to face Dillon, still unsure of exactly what she wanted to do or say—and resigned to the fact that whatever it was it would probably only make things worse—when she spotted Deidre and Blake walking down the opposite side of the street like two angels of mercy.

"Deidre!" she called, waving frantically to get her attention. The instant Deidre looked her way Ivy knew something was wrong. Her skin looked pale, and the way she leaned into Blake gave the distinct impression he was holding her steady.

Forgetting Dillon and every other horrible thing that transpired that morning, she rushed across the street to her cousin. As she drew closer she noticed the bandage on Deidre's forehead.

Her grotesquely *swelled* forehead.

Ivy's horror and surprise must have shown, because the first thing out of Deidre's mouth was, "It's not as bad as it looks."

"Let me see." Without waiting for permission, she lifted Deidre's bangs to get a better look. The area over her left eye looked swollen and tender, and hints of purple peeked out from under the edge of the bandage. "Oh, my God, what happened to you?"

"An alleged golfing mishap," Blake said bitterly.

Deidre ducked away from Ivy and shot him a look. "It was an accident. And the doctor at the clinic said the swelling should be down in time for the wedding."

"You had to see a doctor?"

Deidre nodded. "I needed three stitches."

Why did it have to happen this week? It was just one more thing to put a damper on the most important day of Deidre's life.

"Who did this to you?" Dillon asked, and Ivy jolted

at the sound of his voice. She hadn't even realized he'd followed her.

"Dale's girlfriend," Blake all but spat out. "She swung her club and lost her grip. It went flying and pegged Deidre in the head."

"But it was an accident," Deidre said with a forced cheeriness that wasn't fooling anyone. "Believe me, her aim is not that good. She can barely hit a ball much less a person standing fifteen feet behind her."

Dillon looked from Deidre to Blake. "Which one is Dale's girlfriend? Tweedle Dum or Tweedle Dee?"

Blake shrugged. "Who knows. I can't tell them apart. When it happened, I was more concerned with stopping the bleeding than figuring out who was at fault."

The only thing concerning Ivy was Deidre's pasty-white pallor and the dark circles under her eyes. The way she clung to Blake's arm, as though without him there she might topple over.

Dillon's eyes mirrored Ivy's concern. "Maybe you should go back to the villa and lay down for a while."

"No! I refuse to spend the week of my wedding in bed feeling sorry for myself." Deidre sounded awfully close to tears, and Ivy had the distinct feeling there was more to this than she was admitting. "I don't want to talk about my head anymore."

Blake looked curiously between Ivy and Dillon. "So, what are you guys up to?"

What he really meant was, what were they doing together.

"We were shopping and we bumped into each other," Ivy said, shooting Dillon a look that said she knew damn well their meeting had been no accident. And if he said one word about what had happened, he would die a very slow, agonizing death.

He just smiled. "That's right, and I was just about to invite Ivy to lunch."

"Perfect!" Deidre gushed, perking up instantly. "We were looking for somewhere to eat." She wove an arm through Ivy's and clamped down. Hard. "We can all eat together."

The death grip on Ivy's arm said very clearly that this was not a matter of choice. Ivy was going, even if Deidre had to drag her there.

Seeing there was no way to get out of this without making a scene, and making matters worse in the process, Ivy plastered a smile on her face and said, "Great. Let's eat."

The second they were shown to a table inside the bustling, noisy café, Deidre said something about needing to freshen up, then dragged Ivy with her to the ladies' room. Her grip on Ivy's arm was so tight she was cutting off the circulation. When they were safely inside with the door shut Deidre finally let go.

Ivy shook the blood back into her tingling fingers. "All right, what's going on?"

"I hate them," Deidre spat with a ferocity that was completely unlike her. Angry tears pooled in her eyes. "I hate the Tweedles and I hate Blake's brothers."

Deidre didn't *hate* anybody. She was too sweet. But apparently even she had limits.

"What happened?"

"After I got hit, Blake went to go get the rental car. While he was gone, the four of them were—" Her voice broke and tears dribbled down her cheeks.

Ivy rubbed her shoulder. "They were what? What did they do?"

Deidre sniffled loudly and wiped the tears away with the heels of her palms. "They were…making fun of me. They were whispering and laughing."

Was it possible that they could be that rude? That cruel? "Could you hear what they were saying? I mean, maybe you misunderstood. Maybe they weren't talking about you." As she said the words she suspected they weren't true.

"They were looking right at me, and I heard Dale say it was my own fault for standing too close while she putted."

No, this was *Ivy's* fault. She had been afraid that antagonizing the Tweedles at dinner last night would only make things worse. That they might retaliate. She never should have lowered herself to their level.

And who had encouraged her to do that?

Dillon.

It didn't excuse her behavior. Or make her any less accountable, but in a roundabout way this was as much his fault as hers.

The thought made her feel a little bit better.

"Does Blake know about what they said?"

She sniffled and shook her head. "He already feels so bad. This would only make things worse."

Ivy didn't know if things could get much worse. That would take a tropical storm or a tsunami.

"She didn't even say she was sorry." Deidre wiped her eyes. "What did I ever do to them? Why are they so mean to me?"

"It's not you, Deidre. It's like I said at dinner last night. They're insecure. Cutting you down makes them feel better about themselves." She stepped into one of the empty stalls, pulled a length of toilet paper off the roll and handed it to Deidre. "It's also very possible that they're jealous."

"Yeah right," Deidre said with an indignant snort. She dabbed at her eyes and wiped her nose. "I'm sure they're both dying to be overweight and have my lousy skin. I'm like an ugly duckling next to them."

"It has nothing to do with looks or weight. They're jealous because no matter how skinny they are, or pretty they are, or how blond they dye their hair, they'll never be as happy as you and Blake. Hell, *I'm* jealous and I don't even want to get married."

Deidre shrugged.

"I'm serious. Blake is crazy about you. Anyone can see how happy you two are, how much you love each other. And no matter how mean and nasty the Tweedles are, they can't take that from you."

A grin teased the corners of Deidre's mouth. "You really think they're jealous?"

"I honestly do. Those two may be aesthetically attractive. Maybe even beautiful. But on the inside they're the worst kind of ugly."

"Blake's brothers don't think so."

"They're no better than the Tweedles. I sometimes

wonder how Blake turned out so normal when the rest of his family is completely wacky."

The smile spread to her cheeks. "Wacky? Is that an official diagnosis?"

Ivy laughed. "Absolutely."

Deidre may not have been conventionally beautiful, but she had a warm, genuine smile and a good heart. Ivy hoped Blake realized just how lucky he was.

And maybe somewhere deep down, she *was* a little jealous. But not everyone was lucky enough to find what Deidre and Blake had.

Some people weren't capable.

Deidre wiped her eyes one last time and tossed the tissue in the trash. "You know, no matter how lousy things seem, you always manage to make me feel better."

"It's what I'm trained to do."

"No, it's always been that way, even when we were really little. It's a gift."

If that were true, Ivy wished she could bestow that gift on herself.

"That's the reason I got you and Dillon together," Deidre admitted. "I wanted to help you the way you always help me. I wanted you to be happy."

"I am happy." The words spilled out automatically, but they sounded dry and hollow. Like maybe she wasn't so convinced anymore.

"Speaking of Dillon," Deidre said, "what's *really* going on with you two?"

Ivy shrugged. "Just like I said, we bumped into each other."

"You're sure about that."

Something in Deidre's expression said she knew something Ivy didn't. "Of course I'm sure."

"So what you're telling me is, you were just walking along and accidentally ran into him with your lips?"

Ivy winced.

Oh, crud. Didn't it just figure that not only had her plan backfired, but of the thousands of people roaming the city, Deidre had to be there to witness her mistake.

"Did Blake see?"

"Lucky for you he was looking the other way. And before you ask, no, I didn't say anything to him. And if you ask me not to, I won't. But do not think for a second that I'm going to let you off the hook. I expect an explanation."

Ivy opened her mouth to speak, but no sound came out. She didn't have a clue what to say.

"Well?" Deidre asked, all but tapping her foot, waiting impatiently. "What's the deal?"

"You know, if we don't get to the table soon, the men are going to send in a search party." She made a move toward the door, but Deidre blocked her way.

"I'm not letting you leave until you tell me the truth."

Ivy sighed. She may as well come clean. The worst Deidre could say is I told you so. "Okay, so I kissed him. But I did it to prove I was completely over him. That I'm not attracted to him anymore."

Deidre nodded. "I see. And did it work?"

"Umm…" She bit her lip.

"The truth, Ivy."

"I may have been a little…*flustered.*"

"I saw your face, honey. You were more than a little

flustered. You looked as if you'd gone ten rounds with the ghost of Christmas past."

Okay, so maybe I told you so *wasn't* the worst she could say.

If her feelings had been so clear to Deidre, Dillon must have known exactly what she was feeling. The man always did have an uncanny way of reading her thoughts, her body language.

"Proving that what you said was right," she told Deidre. "I haven't had sex in a long time. Too long, obviously. And it had nothing at all to do with Dillon."

"That's good, Ivy." Deidre reached for the knob and pulled the door open. "If you keep telling yourself that you might start believing it."

Seven

*Want to discover the secret (and dirty!) tactics
men use to make our lives hell?
(Shh...don't tell them we know!)*
—excerpt from *The Modern Woman's Guide to
Divorce (And the Joy of Staying Single)*

The man clung to her like lint on a black wool blazer.

After lunch, which she grudgingly admitted was not
as bad as she'd anticipated, Deidre, Blake and Dillon
took off to sightsee. Ivy headed back to the house and
found it blissfully empty. No Tweedles, no ex-husbands
or neurotic battered brides. Only tranquil silence.

Thirty seconds later Dillon strolled through the door.

She felt like throwing up her hands in surrender,
breaking down and crying, and shoving Dillon over the

balcony, down the rocky bluff and into the ocean below. All at the same time.

Just remember, he's doing this on purpose, she reminded herself. He's doing it to annoy you. Do not let him know it's working.

"I thought you were going sightseeing," she said in a flat, I'm-only-asking-to-be-polite voice.

He just shrugged—a slight hunch of his shoulders and an almost imperceptible tilt of his head. "Changed my mind."

No, he hadn't. This had been the plan all along.

Tease her with a hint of freedom, a few precious moments of peace, before he was back annoying her again.

Despite how many times she brushed him off, cosmic static cling kept drawing him back.

Just like lint.

Only, in this case, a dryer sheet wouldn't be much help. They didn't make one big enough or powerful enough to get rid of someone like him. The way to avoid Dillon, Ivy realized, would be to shut herself away in her room for the remainder of the week.

It couldn't be any worse than spending a week with him.

"I'm going up to my room to rest. I'll see you later." Much, *much* later.

"I understand why you might need some time alone," he said, a devilish glint in his eyes. "That kiss did get you pretty hot and bothered. You go ahead and take care of business."

"Business?" For a second she was confused, then it

hit her. She realized exactly what he meant by *business*. Did he really think she was going upstairs to—

"I have nothing against going solo." He stepped closer, eyes sparking with desire. His voice dropped a few decibels, even though they were the only ones there. "In fact, you might not remember, but I love to watch."

Oh, she remembered.

The things he'd talked her into doing back then still made her blush. Unlike past boyfriends, he'd never played the if-you-loved-me-you-would card. He'd been patient. A tender, generous lover. The kind of man who never failed to put her needs before his own.

The memory poured over Ivy like melted milk chocolate. Rich and sweet and warm. And her head had begun to get that light, fuzzy feeling…

Damn, damn, damn.

He was pulling that sexy, simmering thing he did so well. And like an idiot she was falling for it. *Again!* How could someone she disliked as much as Dillon be so darned appealing? Could it be that she didn't dislike him as much as she thought?

Or was she just losing her mind?

The worst part was he knew it. He knew exactly what he was doing to her, and he was loving every second of it.

Someone needed to cool that man's engines.

Since tossing him over the balcony into the ocean wasn't an option, she would have to settle for the next best thing.

"On second thought, maybe I'll dip my feet in the pool for a second and cool off." She switched direction, heading instead for the French doors that would take her to the pool deck. She knew he would follow, and he didn't disappoint her.

The man's libido had been bound to get him into trouble one of these days. She was just glad she would be around to see him get a dose of his own medicine. And even better, she would be the one to dispense the bitter pill.

He reached past her, like the gentleman he'd always been, and opened the door.

She stepped outside, a wall of dry, sweltering heat drawing her into its grip.

"Damn!" Dillon said. "Sure is hot out here."

Not to worry, he would be cooled off soon enough.

"I could use a cold drink," he said. "Can I get you something?"

"Whatever you're having."

"Two mineral waters comin' right up."

His arrogance, his unshakable self-confidence, would be his undoing.

She walked to the deep end of the pool, hiked her skirt up to the midthigh region so it wouldn't get wet— and hell, why not give him a decent view before he went down—and sat on the edge, the hot tile scorching the backs of her legs. She dipped her feet in and cool water lapped around her ankles. The midday sun reflecting off the surface strobed in her eyes and made her squint.

She watched as Dillon stepped around the bar and fished two bottles of water from the refrigerator. With the exception of a sip of champagne, she still hadn't seen him drink a single alcoholic beverage.

"You don't drink anymore?" she asked.

He opened both waters and added a wedge of lime to each one. "Occasionally."

Keep a casual conversation going so he doesn't suspect, she told herself. Act as if everything is normal. "What made you quit?"

"You ever try to run a billion-dollar corporation with a raging hangover?" He carried them both over to where she sat, and the anticipation was killing her.

"So it was interfering with your work?"

He shrugged. "The truth is, I didn't make a conscious effort to stop. I guess I just outgrew it." He leaned slightly forward to hand her a bottle. "Here you go."

"Thank you." She cast him a bright smile. This was going to feel *so* good.

She reached up to grab it, but instead she wrapped her hand around his wrist and yanked as hard as she could. He teetered for a second, trying to catch his balance, then he laughed and cursed and let himself fall.

He landed with a noisy, messy *kersploosh,* bottles and all, splashing her from head to toe with pool water.

"Yes!" She jumped to her feet, cherishing her victory. Maybe now he would stop messing with her; he would see she meant business. And even if he didn't, it had been a lot of fun.

She gazed down into the water. Any second now, he would rise to the top and see her smug smile, the satisfaction in her eyes. Maybe the kiss idea had been a disaster, but this would be her moment of triumph.

Yep, any second now.

She squinted to make out his shadowy form against the

dark tile lining the bottom of the pool. He was still *way* down there. Maybe he was looking for the water bottles. So someone didn't accidentally step on one and cut their foot. Only thing was, he didn't appear to be moving.

A pocket of air rose and bubbled to the surface but still no Dillon.

What if he'd hurt himself?

No, that was silly. She had seen him go in. He hadn't hit his head or twisted anything. At least, she didn't think so. He was fine. He was just trying to get her to jump in after him.

Well, she wasn't falling for it.

But how long could someone hold their breath? It had already been a while, hadn't it? Close to a minute even. At least it seemed that way.

As every second ticked past, her confidence began to fizzle.

What if there was something really wrong? What if he wasn't breathing? What if he'd been telling the truth and he really didn't know how to swim?

He'd told her he never learned how and she'd pushed him in regardless, meaning she would be responsible if he was hurt.

If he *died*.

Her heart dropped hard and fast, leaving a sick, empty hole in her chest as a dozen gruesome images flashed through her brain at the speed of light. Dillon being dragged from the pool, his tanned skin gray and waxy, his lips a deathly shade of blue.

Dillon's funeral. Having to face his family and admit it had been her fault.

She thought of all the things she could have said to him, *should have said,* and had never gotten the chance.

Her stomach churned with the possibilities, and her head swam with disbelief. She didn't like Dillon, but she didn't want him dead, either.

And what if no one believed it was an accident? She could see the headlines now. *Bestselling author murders ex-husband after publicly berating him in her tell-all book.*

Dillon had floated closer to the surface, but he still wasn't moving, and she was running out of time. There was no way he could hold his breath for that long.

Oh, hell.

She kicked off her sandals and dove in, the cool water swallowing her up like a hungry beast, numbing her senses. All she could feel was the dull throb of panic squeezing her chest, hear the beat of her own pulse in her ears, louder and louder as she descended. She opened her eyes, blinking against the burn of chlorine. Her gaze darted back and forth as she searched, desperate to spot his floating form. She would have to hoist him from the pool and do mouth-to-mouth, get his airway cleared. She'd been certified in first aid and CPR for years, but she'd never actually had to use it. She only hoped she remembered how.

But she would have to find him first. He was gone, as if he had vanished into thin air, or been sucked into an alternate universe.

She hit the bottom at the ten-foot mark and flipped over, her long skirt tangling around her legs. She looked up and saw a pair of booted feet and blue jeans and the lower half of a male torso. The rest of him was out of the water.

And he was very much alive.

She heard a muffled noise above her and realized it was laughter. He was laughing.

He was okay. All this time he'd been okay, and now he was *laughing* at her.

She pushed off the bottom of the pool and sailed to the surface, her lungs screaming for air.

A minute ago all she could think about was saving his sorry behind. Now she wanted to kill him.

Dillon hoisted himself up onto the pool edge beside the ladder, wiping water from his eyes and sweeping his dripping hair back from his forehead. His wet jeans clung to him like a cloying second skin, his boots were toast and his lungs burned like the devil from holding his breath for too long. But it would be worth it. Worth the look on Ivy's face when she resurfaced.

Would she never learn? No matter how dirty she played, he always sank an inch lower. He always won.

Ivy popped up out of the water, blinking rapidly to clear her eyes. Her auburn ponytail hung lopsided and limp and one side of her tank top drooped down her arm.

She looked like a drowned rat.

He smiled and said, "Gottcha."

She didn't yell, didn't call him a jerk. She didn't even look at him. She just swam to the ladder in a few long, easy strokes and grabbed the rail. For a second he thought she might try to dunk him, but she only pulled herself up from the water. Her wet skirt stuck to her legs and was considerably more transparent than it had been before.

Was that a pink thong she was wearing?

Her eyes were rimmed with red, her mouth pulled into a rigid line.

"Hey." He reached out and grabbed her arm but she jerked it away. Without a word she walked across the patio to the house, wet feet slapping, clothes dripping.

He knew every one of Ivy's expressions and he could swear he'd just seen her on-the-verge-of-tears face.

Of all the reactions she could have possibly had, why would she cry? Anger he could understand. He'd expected her to be furious. But tears?

Or maybe she was crying because he *hadn't* drowned.

No. If she'd wanted him dead, she wouldn't have jumped in to rescue him. Maybe she was just embarrassed that once again he had bested her. The gentlemanly thing to do would be to apologize, even though she'd started it, then maybe rub it in her a face one more time for good measure.

He jumped up and went after her, his feet squishing in his sodden boots. "Ivy, hold up."

But she didn't stop moving. If anything, she walked faster. She flung open the door, but, thanks to a much longer stride, he caught her just inside the threshold.

"Come on, Ivy, stop." He reached for her, wrapping his hand around her wrist. Once again she jerked free and marched through the living room. She wasn't just a little angry that he'd gotten the best of her. She was seriously peeved.

"Come on, Ivy, it was a joke. Lighten up."

She stopped abruptly and swung around to face him. Her eyes were bloodshot, her face pale, and tears hovered just inside her eyelids.

"A joke?" she asked incredulously. Her lower lip quivered and her hands were trembling. "You call *that* a joke?"

He shrugged. "I was just fooling around."

"Fooling around?" She took a step toward him, raising both her arms. For a second he thought she was going to deck him, or wrap her hands around his throat and squeeze. Instead she planted both hands on his chest and gave him a good, hard shove. Because he was prepared and outweighed her by almost half, he didn't go very far.

"Fooling around?" she repeated. Then she gave him another shove, harder this time, knocking him back a couple of inches and darn near forcing the air from his lungs. "You scared me to death, you idiot! I thought you drowned! I thought you were *dead.*"

The tears flowed over and rolled down her cheeks, and whatever pride remained of his victory fizzled away. "I didn't mean to scare you."

An explosive combination of fear and fury burned hot and lethal in her eyes. She wound up again, but before she could shove him he grabbed her wrists. She tried to jerk away, but this time he held on.

"Let go of me!" She twisted and yanked, struggling to break free, and he began to worry that she was so hysterical, she would hurt not only him, but herself.

"Ivy, calm down! I didn't mean to scare you." He

pulled her against him, managed to get his arms around her, pinning her close to his body to protect them both. She was cold, wet and trembling all over. *"I'm sorry."*

Eight

Has your ex frustrated you to the breaking point? Physical violence, though tempting, is not the answer. Try a punching bag or a voodoo doll instead.
—excerpt from *The Modern Woman's Guide to Divorce (And the Joy of Staying Single)*

Ivy wrestled with him another second or two, then went still in his arms.

"I'm sorry," he said again, since that seemed to do the trick. He pressed his cheek to the top of her soggy head.

Her body went lax, as if she'd burned up every last bit of energy, and she all but collapsed against him. Her arms circled his waist and she clung to him, a dripping, trembling, emotional catastrophe.

It wasn't supposed to happen this way. The game had gotten way out of hand this time. Hadn't they hurt each other enough?

"I'm sorry," he whispered, and her arms squeezed him tighter. He would say it a million times if it would take back what he'd done.

"I th-thought you were dead," she hiccuped, her cheek pressed against his wet shirt. His throat felt tight with emotion.

Jesus, what was wrong with him?

Maybe it was a little crazy—or a lot crazy—but he liked her this way. Soft and sweet and vulnerable. She was usually so independent, so driven, he'd rarely had the opportunity to play the role of the hero. The protector.

He stroked her soggy, tangled hair, and for one of those brief, fleeting moments remembered all the reasons he'd fallen in love with her. And wondered why in the hell he'd let her get away.

But it was tough to keep someone around who didn't want to be there.

"You're going to wish you had drowned, because when I stop shaking, I'm going to kill you," she warned him, but she didn't let go. Didn't even loosen her grip.

Why would she get so upset if she didn't still care about him, didn't still love him somewhere deep down?

And what difference would it make if she did? They'd had their go-around, and it had been a disaster. They may have loved each other, but that didn't mean they could get along.

That didn't mean there hadn't been good times, too.

He cupped a hand under her chin and lifted her face to his. She gazed up at him with watery, bloodshot eyes, mascara running down her face, and he couldn't stop himself from smiling.

"I must look awful," she said with a sniffle.

He rubbed his thumbs across her cheeks, wiping away the last of her tears. "Not at all."

In fact, he couldn't remember her ever looking more beautiful, more appealing than she did at that very second.

He brushed his thumbs over her full lips. Her mouth looked soft and inviting. He tried to recall what it felt like to kiss her, and not that taunting little peck she'd laid on him earlier. A real, honest to goodness, I'll-go-nuts-if-I-can't-have-you-this-second kiss.

When he looked in her eyes he could swear she was thinking the exact same thing.

In that instant he knew he needed to kiss her. Not wanted. He *needed* to.

It wasn't about revenge or breaking her spirit. It wasn't even about sex. It was just something he *had* to do.

He lowered his head and she rose up to meet him halfway. They came together swift and firm. With purpose. As though they both knew what they wanted and they weren't afraid to take it, the consequences be damned.

She took him into her mouth, against her tongue. She tasted warm and familiar and exciting.

He didn't know what he was expecting, but it wasn't for Ivy to grab his ass and drive herself hard against him. He was so surprised and so turned on, he just about embarrassed himself. He didn't even know it was possible to get a boner wearing ice-cold wet denim.

He bit down on her lip, the way he used to, and she moaned her appreciation. The sound slipped over him like exquisite Italian silk, cranking his level of arousal up yet another notch. Then she slipped her hand between their tightly fused bodies and rubbed it over his crotch, and he was the one moaning.

He knew without a doubt that kissing her was not going to cut it. He needed to get her naked. He wouldn't be satisfied until he was driving himself deep inside her. Watching her shatter in his arms.

He tugged at her soggy shirt, trying to push it up and out of the way, so he could get his hands on some skin. She must have had the same idea, because he could feel her wrestling with the hem of his shirt. At least they were on the same page.

But these wet clothes had to go.

He nipped her lip again, and Ivy moaned. She fisted her hands in his shirt, her nails scraping his skin. Everything in her body language begged, *take me now,* and he couldn't come up with a single reason why he shouldn't. Not that he was trying all that hard to come up with one.

Then he heard a door open and voices in the foyer. An obnoxious, earsplitting cackle of laughter rang through his ears. That was the laugh of a Tweedle. He could feel his hard-on instantly begin to deflate.

Looked as if they were about to have company.

Why the hell hadn't he swept her up and carried her to his room? Or her room. Or the bathroom? *Anywhere* that they would have a little privacy.

As abruptly as they had come together, they broke apart. Both dazed and breathless. And still soaking wet.

Ivy blinked a few times, gazing around as if she'd completely forgotten where she was.

The Tweedles and Blake's brothers appeared in the hallway a second later, like crashers at a private party. *His* party. They were still dressed in their golf gear, and Dee, or was it Dum—he still couldn't tell them apart—was laughing. Awfully jovial, weren't they, considering what had happened to Deidre?

He absently wondered which one had pegged her, and if she felt even a modicum of regret. If she cared about anyone but herself.

All four stopped abruptly when they noticed Ivy and Dillon standing there. The one he was pretty sure was Dum inspected them from head toe, a look of revulsion on her face. "Oh, my God. What happened to you?"

Ivy looked from Dillon, to herself, then back to their captivated audience. He couldn't wait to see how she explained this one.

She shrugged, the picture of innocence, and said, "We went swimming." As if that was obvious, and not at all unusual despite the fact that they were both fully dressed.

She always did have a way of making the ridiculous or unlikely seem completely rational.

Not that he gave a damn what the four Musketeers did or didn't know.

Of course, at some point the news would have gotten back to his mother. He didn't really give a damn what she thought, either. But the business of trying to explain and assuring her that there was no way in hell he and

Ivy would ever try to reconcile would be a big pain in the behind. A hassle he didn't need. Or want.

If they were going to do this, it would be best to keep it to themselves.

And they were. Even if Ivy didn't realize it yet.

"You're dripping everywhere," the other Tweedle said, mirroring her counterpart's distaste.

Those two really needed to lighten up.

Ivy looked down at the growing puddle of water around her feet. "Oops. Guess I should go change into some dry clothes."

Gathering her wet skirt, she bolted for the stairs, but not before he saw the mildly shocked, what-the-hell-have-I-done look on her face.

"Guess I should change, too," Dillon said, heading after her, leaving the others looking thoroughly confused.

"Who's going to clean up this mess?" one of the Tweedles called after him, but he was more concerned with the pound of Ivy's footsteps up the stairs. She was moving awfully fast.

By the time he reached the foot of the stairs she was already at the top.

"Ivy, wait," he called to her, but either she didn't hear him or she was ignoring him.

He was guessing the latter.

She disappeared down the hall and a second later he heard her bedroom door slam. From where he stood he couldn't actually hear her turn the lock but knew that she had.

It didn't take a genius to realize she was running away again.

* * *

Dillon was worse than lint, Ivy decided as she stepped out of the shower into the steamy bathroom and dried off with a soft, fluffy orange towel. She'd scrubbed and scrubbed, run the water as hot as she could stand, and she could still feel the ghost of his touch. She could still smell his scent on her skin.

She'd brushed her teeth twice and rinsed with mouthwash, but she could still taste him.

He wasn't just clinging to her sleeve or the leg of her slacks. He was under her skin, coursing through her bloodstream. She could feel him inside her head, making things she used to believe, things she counted on, hazy and unclear.

She rubbed the steam from a section of the mirror and looked at herself. Really looked. Same hair, same eyes, same nothing special body.

Then why did she feel so…*different?*

Confused and frustrated and scared…and more *alive* than she had in years.

She slipped her robe on and opened the bathroom door, letting out a startled squeak when she realized she wasn't alone.

No, Dillon wasn't lint.

He was a virus. A full-blown flu that made her feel weak and feverish and blew her judgment all to hell. A highly contagious bug who had broken into her room while she showered and made himself comfortable on her bed.

"Howdy." He lay on his back, propped up on both elbows, one leg crossed over the other. Like he had every right to be there. He'd showered and changed into casual slacks and a slightly transparent, white linen pullover that all but screamed, look at my tan! The scent of freshly scrubbed man reached across the room and wrapped itself around her like a tentacle, tempting her closer.

Did viruses have tentacles?

She tugged the belt on her robe a little tighter. Just in case.

She didn't trust Dillon, and even worse, she didn't trust herself. That kiss downstairs would have knocked her out of her shoes had she been wearing any. She never thought the day would come when she would say she was happy to see the Tweedles, but thank goodness they had walked in, jaws flapping. They were the only thing that had stopped her from making another huge mistake.

"Good shower?" Dillon asked, looking her up and down with warm, blue bedroom eyes.

Every one of her billion or so nerve endings went on full alert. Her brain kicked into overdrive to compensate and threatened a complete shutdown.

Why in the hell had she kissed him again? Hadn't she learned her lesson the first time? Hadn't she learned it *ten* stinking years ago?

The lack of oxygen from staying under the water so long had clearly damaged her brain.

Or maybe he really was a virus, and she just didn't have the antibodies to fight him off.

"I know I locked the door before I got in the shower," she said, doing her best to sound stern. So he wouldn't know that she was thinking of how much better he would look out of his clothes than in them.

He looked at the door, then back to her. "What's your point?"

Could he be more arrogant? Any cooler or more composed? More of a pain in the behind?

"A closed, locked door generally means the person on the other side doesn't want to be disturbed."

He just grinned. The frustratingly charming grin she both loved and hated. She would order him to leave if she thought he would actually listen. Hell, she'd even try hosing him down with Lysol. But she knew it was a futile battle. All the disinfectant and antibiotics in the world wouldn't fend him off. Like every other virus she'd had, he would simply have to run his course.

This time she wouldn't give in and let him become a full-blown epidemic.

She shoved her wet, tangled hair back from her eyes. "Do I even want to know how you got the door unlocked?"

He reached into the pocket of his slacks and pulled out a credit card. "I used my Visa."

So much for her plan of staying barricaded in her room for the rest of a trip. Not even a locked door could keep him out. Besides, wouldn't that be like letting him win?

This game he was playing was getting more complicated by the hour. It would be so much easier if she knew the rules, but she had the uneasy suspicion that there weren't any.

She tried to work up the enthusiasm to be annoyed but didn't see the point. Her anger was wasted on him. If anything, he seemed to enjoy getting her riled up. "Was there something you wanted?"

He flashed her that sexy, simmering grin and wiggled his eyebrows. "You know what I want, darlin'."

Oh, *that*. And here she had been hoping he wanted to play checkers.

Then he—*Oh, my God*—pulled his shirt over his head and dropped it on the bed beside him.

Hunk alert.

All that bronzed skin and lean muscle was making her eyes cross.

He patted the mattress. "Why don't you slip out of that robe and squeeze in here beside me."

If only he knew how tempting that was.

The bedroom was the one place he had never disappointed her. And it wasn't just the sex, although, Lord knew that had been out-of-this-world marvelous. But, being something of a nerd, one of her favorite things had been to just talk. Back then, few people had had the privilege of meeting the intellectually intriguing man lost behind the rebellious, party-boy facade. Some nights they had made love for hours, then had lain awake until dawn discussing social issues and politics and world events.

She wondered when that had stopped. When going out to the bar with his buddies had become more appealing than spending time with her. When the discussions had turned into arguments, the arguments to angry sex. Until even that had no longer been able to connect them. Until they had been just plain angry.

When she didn't move, he sighed and let his head fall back. His neck was lean and tanned, and she could see a tiny mark under his chin where he'd nicked himself

The Silhouette Reader Service™ — Here's how it works:

Accepting your 2 free books and 2 free mystery gifts places you under no obligation to buy anything. You may keep the books and gifts and return the shipping statement marked "cancel". If you do not cancel, about a month later we'll send you 6 additional books and bill you just $3.80 each in the U.S. or $4.47 each in Canada, plus 25¢ shipping & handling per book and applicable taxes if any.* That's the complete price and — compared to cover prices of $4.50 each in the U.S. and $5.25 each in Canada — it's quite a bargain! You may cancel at any time, but if you choose to continue, every month we'll send you 6 more books, which you may either purchase at the discount price or return to us and cancel your subscription.

If offer card is missing write to: Silhouette Reader Service, 3010 Walden Ave., P.O. Box 1867, Buffalo NY 14240-1867

NO POSTAGE
NECESSARY
IF MAILED
IN THE
UNITED STATES

BUSINESS REPLY MAIL

FIRST-CLASS MAIL   PERMIT NO. 717   BUFFALO, NY

POSTAGE WILL BE PAID BY ADDRESSEE

SILHOUETTE READER SERVICE
3010 WALDEN AVE
PO BOX 1867
BUFFALO NY 14240-9952

GET FREE BOOKS and FREE GIFTS WHEN YOU PLAY THE...

SLOT MACHINE GAME!

Just scratch off the silver box with a coin. Then check below to see the gifts you get!

YES! I have scratched off the silver box. Please send me the 2 free Silhouette Desire® books and 2 free gifts for which I qualify. I understand I am under no obligation to purchase any books, as explained on the back of this card.

326 SDL ELYM   225 SDL ELQA

FIRST NAME   LAST NAME

ADDRESS

APT.#   CITY

STATE/ PROV.   ZIP/POSTAL CODE

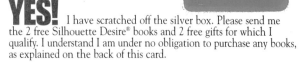

7	7	7	**Worth TWO FREE BOOKS plus 2 BONUS Mystery Gifts!**
🍒	🍒	🍒	**Worth TWO FREE BOOKS!**
♣	♣	🍒	**Worth ONE FREE BOOK!**
🔔	🔔	🍒	**TRY AGAIN!**

www.eHarlequin.com

(S-D-05/07)

Offer limited to one per household and not valid to current Silhouette Desire® subscribers.

Your Privacy - Silhouette Books is committed to protecting your privacy. Our Privacy Policy is available online at www.eHarlequin.com or upon request from the Silhouette Reader Service. From time to time we make our lists of customers available to reputable firms who may have a product or service of interest to you. If you would prefer for us not to share your name and address, please check here ☐.

shaving. "Is it safe to assume that we're not going to pick up where we left off downstairs?"

"What happened downstairs was a mistake." A huge, monster-size, "ginormous" mistake.

"Wouldn't be my first, and I doubt it'll be my last."

"That doesn't justify what we did. It's pretty obvious we have some unresolved issues, but I don't think hopping into bed is the way to fix them."

Not that it wouldn't be fun.

He flashed her that hungry, devilish grin. "The only thing unresolved between us is that we still make each other hot. And hopping into bed together, right here, right now, is the perfect way to fix that."

"Maybe that was the problem with our marriage. Maybe it was only about the sex."

"Who could blame us, since we did it so well."

She shot him a look. One he would no doubt recognize as exasperation. "I'm serious, Dillon."

"So am I." He reached over and pulled back the covers. "Come here, I'll remind you."

She just stood there, arms folded over her chest. He blew out an exasperated breath and fell back against the pillow. It was so typically Dillon, so familiar, her heart ached the tiniest bit.

"Darlin', you're sending so many mixed signals I'm getting whiplash. Did you or did you not kiss me? Twice in fact."

"Call it temporary insanity. Let me say this loud and clear so there's no confusion. We are not having sex. Not today, not tomorrow, not ten years from now."

"How about Saturday? Could we do it then?"

"Never."

He considered that for a second, then asked, "When you say sex, do you mean intercourse only, or are you lumping foreplay in there, too?"

She wasn't going to justify that with a response. "No wonder our marriage went to hell. You can't be serious for two seconds."

A muscle in his jaw twitched, and she knew she'd hit a sore spot. She seemed to have a knack for doing that. "How's this for serious? I can tell you *exactly* why our marriage went to hell. You didn't trust me."

So, they were back to blaming her. How typical. And to think that only a few minutes ago she had seriously been considering sleeping with him. "If I didn't trust you, Dillon, I had a damn good reason. You weren't exactly reliable."

"Reliable?" Now he looked downright resentful. "Did I ever make you a promise I didn't keep?"

She wanted to be able to say yes. But the honest truth was, he'd never broken a promise. When he gave his word, he'd never failed to follow through. The tricky part was getting him to make the promise in the first place.

Did that make him unreliable or self-centered? Or simply smart enough to know his own limitations?

And what difference did it make now?

"No," she admitted. "You never made a promise you didn't keep, but like always, you're grossly oversimplifying. It wasn't about lies or broken promises. In all the time we were together you never once showed an ounce of incentive. A drive to succeed."

"How do you figure?"

Was he kidding? "Dillon, you were flunking out of school! All you did was drink and gamble."

He shrugged. "So?"

So? Was that all he had to say? Just *so?* "You had so much potential. You could have gone so far."

"*Could have?* I run a billion-dollar corporation, Ivy. How much further did you expect me to go?"

"You know what I mean," she said, although he did have a point. But turning out okay despite his behavior didn't make it right. It just meant he was lucky.

"What I know, Ivy, is that my future was set. My parents had been priming me since the day I was born. I knew that when my dad retired I would take his place. You may find this hard to swallow, but I considered it an honor. One I took *very* seriously."

He sat up, closer now. Too close. His eyes serious. It was unsettling because Dillon didn't do serious very often. "But, damn it, if I was going to be chained to that company for most of my adult life, I was *not* going to spend my youth with my nose buried in a textbook. I was going to have fun."

"How was I supposed to know that?"

"You *did* know that. You knew it because I told you a thousand times. Every time you rode me because I skipped class, or blew off studying to hit a party. I never lied to you, I never made a promise I didn't keep. I never gave you a reason to not believe what I said was true, but that wasn't good enough for you. Which brings us right back to where we started. You. Didn't. Trust. Me."

He was turning everything around, making it look like it was her fault.

Maybe he was right. Maybe she hadn't trusted him completely. But it was more complicated than that. "You may not have given me a reason to mistrust you," she told him, "but trust has to be earned. You have to *make* promises to keep them."

"If you didn't trust me, Ivy, why the hell did you marry me?"

"I wish I hadn't!" she shot back, regretting the words instantly. It was one thing to be angry, but that comment had been downright mean. A vicious low blow.

Dillon gave her this look. Not cold or warm, annoyed or insulted. His face was a blank page. A blank page in a book whose language she had never been able to translate. "I'm real sorry to hear that our life together was such a disappointment for you."

Awkward silence echoed through the room like thunder.

It had happened again. No matter how hard they tried, they just couldn't seem to get along. As usual, nothing had been resolved.

Their relationship was like a long string of Christmas lights rolled up in one big, knotted ball. There was a very short beginning and a sharp, stubby end, but the middle part was so densely tangled and riddled with missing bulbs, she wasn't sure if they could ever make sense of it.

Maybe they weren't meant to resolve anything. Maybe the trick was to throw the old set out and shop for a new one. Or stop hanging the lights altogether, even if it did make life drab and colorless at times. Boring even.

Boring, but safe.

The air was thick and sticky with tension, and she had no idea what to say to him. Thankfully, Deidre chose that second to knock on the door.

Nine

*Move forward and don't look back. The best part
of your life lies ahead. Life's not about the desti-
nation, it's about the journey.*
—excerpt from *The Modern Woman's Guide to
Divorce (And the Joy of Staying Single)*

"Hey, Ivy, you in there?"

"Come in," Ivy called. Deidre's timing couldn't have
been more perfect.

The doorknob jiggled and she said, "It's locked."

She shot Dillon a look. He had broken in, then relocked
the door? The man gave himself far too much credit.

She crossed the room and let her cousin in. Deidre
looked considerably better than she had earlier. The
color had returned to her cheeks, and she'd lost that

muddled, slightly dazed expression. She always had been quick to bounce back.

"I can't find Dillon and I was wondering—" She spotted Dillon lounging on the bed. "Oh! There you are."

Curiosity leaped like wild flames in her eyes, but she played it cool. Ivy could just imagine what she must be thinking. Dillon half-naked on her bed, Ivy in her robe.

It looked pretty bad.

He didn't even have the decency to look guilty or uncomfortable. Or maybe that was a good thing, since they had no reason to feel either. As useless as this conversation had turned out to be, it hadn't been in any way inappropriate. "Yes, ma'am."

"The tailor is here to do the final fitting on the tuxedos. They're waiting for you in the master suite downstairs."

He pulled himself to his feet. "Guess I should get down there."

Taking his time, he grabbed his shirt, turned it right side in, then pulled it over his head. There was something hypnotizing about a man getting dressed, the easy flex and pull of muscle. Yards of smooth skin.

Too bad it wasn't anyone but him.

He crossed the room to the door, but instead of leaving, he stopped. Right by Ivy. He stood there, closer than she was comfortable with. Close enough to look suggestive and raise even more questions.

Which was probably what he wanted. It was probably his way of getting back at her for hitting so far below the belt. She would apologize, but really, hadn't he brought it on himself? Wasn't he the one following her around, breaking into her room, harassing her?

And if that was true, why did she feel so guilty?

Their eyes locked, and his gaze was so intense she could swear he was seeing straight through her skin to her insides. And for some stupid reason she couldn't look away.

Could he really see inside her? And if so, could he see how bad she felt? Did he know that she wanted to apologize?

He leaned toward her the tiniest bit, tilted his head a fraction, and for one brief, horrifying, *exhilarating* second she thought he was going to kiss her. Right in front of her cousin. Her pulse began to race and her mouth went dry.

Explaining to Deidre why they were in her room together, and getting her to believe it, would be difficult enough.

She stood there frozen, holding her breath, waiting to see what he would do. If he would make matters worse.

"It's been…*enlightening,*" he finally said, then turned and walked out.

She didn't really see how he considered this interlude enlightening. Nothing had been resolved. Nothing was *going* to be resolved. Not until he took responsibility for his actions and stopped blaming everything on her. And she knew that would never happen.

Deidre waited several seconds, until they could hear the sound of his footsteps on the stairs, then she shut the door and turned to Ivy. "Enlightening?"

"It's not what you think," Ivy said.

"I'm not sure what I should think."

"Nothing was going on. We were just talking."

"Talking? Oh, my gosh!" Deidre squealed. "That's so awesome!"

No. Not really. "I was trying to take your advice. I wanted to resolve whatever it is we're still hanging on to."

"And?" she pressed, her eyes bright and enthusiastic. And so full of hope it nearly broke Ivy's heart.

Deidre was so excited, Ivy hated to disappoint her. But as her mother used to say, part of growing up is accepting disappointment and realizing that there are some things you just can't change.

When it came to Ivy and Dillon's relationship, Deidre would have to learn to live with defeat.

Ivy had.

"We don't seem to be making much progress." Maybe they weren't meant to resolve anything. Maybe what they needed was to simply forget the past and go their separate ways.

Tough to do when the guy followed her everywhere.

"But you're trying," she gushed, undeterred. She took both of Ivy's hands and squeezed them. "That's what's important. I know that you guys will work things out!"

Ivy wished she could share Deidre's optimism, but it was tough to resolve anything with a man who refused to admit he may have made a mistake.

Dillon didn't say two words to her at dinner.

That had been what she'd wanted all along. For him to leave her alone. So why did she feel so lousy?

Clearly it was the I-wish-I'd-never-married-you statement coming back to bite her in the behind. Not only had it been mean and uncalled for, it wasn't the least bit true.

For every good day, they may have had two lousy ones. And if she had a dime for every night she'd cried herself to sleep she could buy herself a Mercedes.

But if not for Dillon, for their marriage—the good and the bad—she wouldn't be the person she was today. She was stronger because of him. She may have learned the hard way, but she knew how to take care of herself. To beat any odds.

And for some stupid reason she couldn't bring herself to tell him so.

The men went for a guys' night out that evening while the women had the final fittings for their dresses. Six months ago Deidre had gone through fifty different styles of bridesmaid dresses before the Tweedles would agree on one they'd be willing to be seen in. And as Ivy spun in front of the mirror she had to admit the color and design were flattering. Not just flattering, but sexy.

She wondered what Dillon would think. If he would like the way she looked.

Not that she cared, of course.

"Gorgeous!" the seamstress gushed after making a slight adjustment to the spaghetti strap. Of course the Tweedles' size ones were a perfect fit. They were like Stepford bridesmaids. Only scarier.

"We need our bride!" the seamstress called impatiently in the direction of the master bath, where Deidre had disappeared to put on her dress. She had been in there an awfully long time.

The bathroom door opened a crack and Deidre called back, "Ivy, I need you for a minute." Then it slammed shut again.

The seamstress sighed loudly while Dee and Dum exchanged an exasperated look.

"At this rate we're going to be here all night!" Dum groaned.

"I'll see what the problem is," Ivy told them. She lifted the skirt of her dress, so it wouldn't drag on the floor as she crossed the room. She knocked lightly on the door. "Deidre? You okay?"

The door opened and a disembodied hand shot out. It latched on to Ivy's arm and yanked her inside. She barely had time to pull her skirt in before Deidre shut and locked the door.

With her free hand Deidre was holding her partially fastened dress up, clutching the bodice to her breasts. Her face and chest were flushed and beads of sweat dribbled down the sides of her face and into her cleavage. She looked as though she'd just run a marathon.

"What's wrong?" Ivy asked. "The natives are getting restless out there."

Tears hovered just inside her eyelids. "I'm too fat."

Ivy sighed. Not this again. "You are not too fat. You're going to look beautiful."

"No," she insisted. "I mean I'm really too fat." She turned, showing Ivy her back, and the gap between the two sides of the dress between the zipper. "I can't get the dress zipped up."

Oh, crap.

"I pulled and pulled until I heard the fabric start to rip."

Yep. Ivy could see a small tear where the lace had begun to pull away from the silk.

Double crap.

"What am I going to do?" she half whispered, half shrieked. "I can't go out there like this. If Blake's mom finds out it doesn't fit she will *kill* me! This thing cost a fortune!"

In Deidre's defense, Blake's mom was the one who had insisted Deidre order a size smaller, assuring her that it would be a perfect fit after she lost a few pounds. At least at the last fitting she'd been able to zip it up all the way. She'd have been fine if she didn't eat, or move. Or *breathe*.

As far as Ivy was concerned Blake's mother was getting exactly what she deserved for being such a demanding, controlling twit. But Ivy *did not* want to see Deidre unhappy.

"Turn around," she ordered and her cousin complied, her lip clamped so hard between her teeth Ivy worried she might bite clear through. "Don't worry. We'll make it fit."

She grasped the zipper tag. It was slightly disfigured from the workout Deidre had given it. "I want you to inhale and suck it in as far as you can. You ready?"

She nodded.

"On the count of three. One...two...three!"

Deidre sucked, and Ivy pulled for all she was worth. Deidre grunted as Ivy managed to get her zipped about halfway. Then there was an earsplitting rip, and the zipper tag popped loose and flew across the bathroom.

The little tear was now a gaping hole.

Oh, shit.

"That sounded bad," Deidre said, her voice small and frightened.

"It was bad." Ivy was no expert, but she was pretty sure it would take at least an inch of fabric to fix it.

At *least*.

There was no way this dress was going to fit Deidre by Saturday. It wouldn't fit by next week, either. She would have to starve herself and work out nonstop for a month just to get it zipped up.

Ivy had to wonder if all this was worth it. All this frustration and compromise, just to be married.

Not for her. She liked being single and intended to keep it that way.

There was a loud bang on the door. "Are you planning on staying in there until the wedding?" Dee snapped.

All the color had drained from Deidre's face and her eyes were wide with terror. "What am I going to do?" she whispered.

Ivy didn't know, but they had to do *something*. Deidre started to hyperventilate and her face was ashen.

"Give us a few minutes!" Ivy shouted back, and told her cousin, "Relax. We'll figure out something."

Deidre started to cry. Big, fat tears ran down her cheeks. "This is an omen."

"Everything will work out," she assured her, but Deidre wasn't listening.

"This whole stupid week, my whole *life* has been one big, bad omen!"

"Deidre, shh—"

"And I hate this stupid dress!" she shrieked. She tugged it down and shoved it to the floor then proceeded to stomp it flat with her bare feet. "I've hated it from the second that witch forced me into picking it."

Oh, jeez. The stress was too much. It had finally happened. She had come completely unglued.

There was another loud bang on the door. "We're waiting!"

Deidre snatched the dress from the bathroom floor and, wearing only panties and a strapless push-up bra, ripped open the door.

"Here I am! Are you happy?"

Ivy cringed and followed her out. There wasn't much she could do at this point. Other than hold Deidre back if she tried to strangle one of the twins.

The Tweedles stood there in their identical size one dresses with identical stunned looks on their faces.

"Yes, I'm fat!" Deidre all but screamed at them, wild-eyed and sweaty, spinning in a circle so they got the full view. "Does that make you feel better?"

The seamstress looked downright frightened. Apparently she'd never seen a bride-to-be have a total nervous breakdown. She flinched and cowered when Deidre thrust the tattered, wrinkled dress at her.

"This dress does not fit me. I wear a size sixteen. Not a fourteen, not a twelve. A *sixteen*. Find me a size sixteen or I will hurt you. Understand?"

The seamstress nodded, her head wobbling on her neck like one of those bobble-head dogs in a car window. She grabbed the dress and scurried out of the room. The Tweedles, their pea-size brains apparently sensing danger, weren't far behind her.

Then it was just Ivy and Deidre.

Deidre sat on the edge of the bed looking shell-shocked. "I can't do this. I thought I could, but I can't."

Ivy wasn't sure what *this* was. If she meant she couldn't go through with this particular wedding, or if she couldn't marry Blake at all. And honestly, she was afraid to ask.

"Do you know what I need?" she asked.

Wow. The list was so long Ivy wasn't sure where to begin. But if she had to pick one thing, she would start with Valium. "What do you need?"

"I need chocolate. Lots and lots of chocolate."

It took two hours and an entire box of Ho Hos to calm Deidre down. By the time the men returned, Ivy had managed to get her into her pajamas and tucked into bed. And thanks to one of the emergency sleeping pills Ivy kept on hand, she was resting peacefully.

She explained to Blake what had happened.

"What should I do?" he asked, looking so hopelessly baffled she wanted to hug him. She had several suggestions, but it would be better if Blake figured this one out on his own. He'd gone too long letting people run his life for him.

He needed to grow up.

Or Deidre needed to find herself a new future husband.

"Deidre isn't feeling well," Blake announced the next morning at breakfast, when he came to the table alone. His brothers and the Tweedles looked from him, then to each other, and snickered. Didn't they feel the least bit guilty for what had happened? Didn't they realize they had pushed Deidre just a little too far this time?

She'd been balancing precariously on the edge of a cliff, and they had poked and prodded until she'd finally lost her balance and gone over it.

Dillon stood in the kitchen, coffee mug in hand, quietly observing. He still hadn't said a word to Ivy, but she could feel him there, watching her. Yet every time she glanced up, he was looking the other way. Either he was trying to make her feel uncomfortable, or it was her own guilty conscience gnawing at her.

"Is there anything I can do?" Ivy asked Blake.

"I don't think so. The week has been pretty…stressful. I think she just needs some time to rest."

Blake was living in the land of Deep Denial if he thought Deidre could *rest* this one away. He was going to have to face the fact that he needed to make some changes.

If he didn't, he was going to lose Deidre.

"She said you guys should take the boat tour without us. It starts at eleven."

Six hours trapped on a boat sailing up and down the coast with Blake's brothers, the Tweedles and Dillon. *Don't think so.*

"I wouldn't feel right going without her," Ivy said.

Blake shrugged. "The charter is already paid for and it's too late to get a refund. It would be a waste not to use it."

"We made other plans," Dale said, but he wouldn't look his brother in the eye. Blake just shook his head. How many more ways could they let him down this week?

"Ivy and I will go," Dillon said.

She was about to say, *I will?* But she had to wonder if this was his way of saying no hard feelings. And if she said no, what message would that send to him?

Besides, if the charter was nonrefundable, it was a shame to see all that money go to waste. And Deidre might feel better knowing that Ivy and Dillon were taking some time alone together and could potentially work things out.

Not that Ivy thought there was a chance in hell they ever would.

Blake shot her a questioning look. Normally she wouldn't tolerate anyone telling her what to do, but in this case she would make an exception.

"Sure," she told Blake. "We'll go."

Ten

Most women are brought up to believe that their husband will take care of them for the rest of their lives. But that's only true 50% of the time. The other 50% end in divorce.
—excerpt from *The Modern Woman's Guide to Divorce (And the Joy of Staying Single)*

Ivy was flirting.

Shamelessly flirting with a member of the crew. A kid who looked as though he was barely out of high school. Or maybe still in high school for all Dillon knew. Since they'd left the marina she had been cozying up to him, and the kid was practically drooling over her form-fitting tank top and short-shorts.

Okay, maybe the shorts weren't *that* short, but they seemed to show an awful lot of leg.

She'd worn her hair down, and it rested in soft chestnut waves on her shoulders and tumbled down her back to just above her bra strap. Everything about her screamed *pick me up.*

Since Ivy was not, and never had been, the type to flirt—she was way too uptight—Dillon guessed this little show was entirely for his benefit. To make him jealous. Though he had no idea why she thought he would be. Because he wasn't.

At all.

She'd made her feelings pretty damn clear yesterday. She regretted ever marrying him. Wasn't that just great.

Well, it hadn't been all roses and sunshine for him, either. Did she think she'd been easy to live with? Always complaining, her panties always in a twist over something. If she thought he gave a damn what she felt about their marriage, she was mistaken.

And people wondered why he stayed single. Sheesh!

It had been her idea to "talk." Her telling him they needed to resolve things. Far as he could figure, she was pretty gung ho about *resolving* things, until she heard something she didn't like.

He was all for working things out, but how could they if she refused to admit she was wrong?

He had the feeling they were just going to have to agree to disagree and leave it at that. He would go his way and she would go hers and they could forget they ever knew each other.

Although he had to admit, it would have been really nice getting her under the covers one last time.

When they reached the dock later that afternoon, he saw Ivy slip her new boyfriend what appeared to be a business card. It looked as though the lovebirds planned to hook up later. Did she have the slightest clue how ridiculous a woman her age would look dating an adolescent? Did she have no dignity?

He had dated a lot of women in the past couple of years, but never one young enough to be his daughter. Or at the very least, a young niece.

A car waited to take them back to the villa. As they were rolling out of the parking lot he said, "Looks like you made a new friend today."

Ivy cast him a sideways glance, a grin on her face. "You could say that."

Didn't she see how foolish she looked? Pining over some kid. And obviously the kid in question was only in it to get some tail. And what a fine tail it was, he couldn't help noticing.

But that was beside the point.

In college, Ivy had always had been on the naive side. She probably had no clue this kid was using her. She was not the type to settle for a one-night stand. She'd made Dillon wait three excruciating months before she would sleep with him.

Maybe he should point out the obvious and save her a bit of humiliation.

"You don't think he's a little young for you?" he asked.

She was looking out the car window, but he could see her smile widen a fraction. "Just the way I like 'em."

"I hate to break it to you, but he's only after one thing. When you leave Mexico, you'll never hear from him again."

She turned to him, her expression blank. "What's your point?"

She wasn't fooling him with her casual attitude. "I know you, Ivy. You don't do casual. You're a commitment kinda' girl."

She shrugged. "Go ahead and tell yourself that if it makes you feel better."

"This has nothing to do with me. I don't care what you do. I just don't want to see you get your pretty little heart broken."

"I think men should be like tissues," she said. "Soft, strong and disposable. The jealousy is flattering, though."

He snorted. "Jealous of what? You're a complete pain in the ass."

"Maybe, but you still want to sleep with me." She looked over at him. "Admit it."

Great, now she was stealing his material. "Why would I want to sleep with a woman who regrets marrying me?"

Only after the words were out did he realize how pathetic that sounded. Like she'd hurt his feelings or something.

Which she hadn't. He didn't give a damn what she thought about their marriage.

She looked out the window and said in a soft voice, "I didn't mean it."

Was that some sort of veiled apology from Miss Perfection? Miss I'm-Never-Wrong. "You didn't mean what?"

She fiddled with the strap of her purse, eyes downward. "As bad as things got between us, there were good times, too."

"What are you trying to say, Ivy?"

She took a deep breath, looked up and met his eyes. "I'm trying to say that I'm sorry. I'm sorry if I hurt your feelings."

He waited for a sarcastic remark, a caustic dig to pop into his head. Instead he was drawing a blank.

What the hell was wrong with him?

Ivy was proud, so he knew that hadn't been easy for her. He settled for, "You didn't, but apology accepted."

"He's a twenty-two-year-old psychology major," she said, and it took him a second to realize she was talking about the cupcake on the tour. "Really smart kid. He's engaged to a lovely girl that he is absolutely crazy about and plans to marry after they both graduate. They're considering moving to Texas. I told him to give me a call when and if he's ever looking for an internship."

"A bit of advice. Next time you might want to tone down the flirting."

"I was not flirting."

"I saw you, darlin'. You were most definitely flirting, and laying it on thick."

"Okay, maybe a little. But you were jealous. Admit it."

"If I say yes, will you sleep with me?"

She just grinned and turned back to the window. "I knew you were jealous."

He didn't see any point in arguing. Once she set her mind to something she rarely backed down. And what the hell, maybe he had been a *little* jealous.

If anyone was going to sleep with Ivy on this trip, damn it, it was going to be him.

When they got back to the villa everyone else was gone. Since dinner had already been prepared, they figured it would only be polite to sit down and eat. And it wasn't so bad.

Ivy would go so far as to say it was darn near pleasant. Something strange had happened on the ride back from the marina. The tension that had been dogging them since their fight yesterday afternoon seemed to wither away. They seemed to have come to some sort of understanding.

And she began to think that when he followed her around, incessantly bugging her tonight, it might not be such a bad thing. Since there wasn't much else to do.

After dinner he pushed back his chair and stood. "I'm going to call it a night and head up to my room."

Sure he was. "It's barely eight o'clock."

"I'm a little tired, and I have some work I wanted to catch up on."

Did he really think she was that gullible? That she didn't know exactly what he was up to? He was pulling the same routine he always did. He would pretend he was going to leave her alone, then dog her relentlessly all night.

But just to make him happy, she played along. "I guess I'll see you tomorrow, then. Sweet dreams."

Dillon walked around the table, stopped beside her chair and held out his hand. She looked at it suspiciously. He stood there patiently waiting, and finally she slipped her hand in his. She assumed he meant to escort her from the table. Instead he turned her hand over, exposing her wrist, and he leaned forward.

Unsure of what he was doing, but curious to find out, she sat motionless. Even though her heart had begun pounding out a faster and slightly erratic rhythm.

His eyes closed and he inhaled the scent of the perfume she'd dabbed there. The bottle she'd bought in town yesterday.

He looked up at her, his eyes like a hot spring ready to bubble over. "I like it."

Her hand felt small and warm wrapped in his and his breath was hot on her skin. Then his lips brushed just below her palm and tiny jolts of awareness, like little static shocks, rippled up her arm.

Oh, my God.

She found herself looking forward to the time he would spend nagging her, and figured, if today was like every other day this week, she wouldn't have to wait long.

He let go of her hand, then walked inside. She didn't doubt that he'd be back in a minute or two. He would find some ridiculous reason he should keep himself glued to her side.

Yep, *any* minute now.

She sat at the table several minutes, then got up and walked to the balcony railing and looked out over the ocean, at the sun sinking slowly below the horizon. Several minutes passed before she heard a noise behind her.

She couldn't help grinning. The man was *so* predictable.

She wiped the smile from her face and turned to him. "I thought you were going to—" The words trailed off when she realized it wasn't Dillon, but the housekeeper, preparing to clear the table.

"Ma'am?" she asked in a thick Mexican accent.

Ivy's cheeks blushed with embarrassment. "Sorry. I thought you were…someone else."

She scurried past her into the house. The poor woman must have thought she was a loon. Although, compared to Deidre, who scarfed chocolate and had nervous breakdowns, and Dillon, who walked around in his underwear with his winkie hanging out, and the Tweedles—she wouldn't even go there—Ivy was definitely one of the most normal of the bunch.

Apparently Dillon was going to wait until Ivy went to her room, or maybe he was there already, lounging on her bed. The way he had been when she got out of the shower.

That was probably it. All this time she'd been waiting for him, he was probably waiting for her.

She headed up to her room, making sure her footsteps were just heavy enough, so he would know she was coming. The hallway was quiet and dim. Her bedroom door was open, just the way she'd left it, the room dark. No doubt he was going to try to startle her again.

She stepped in the room and switched on the light, eyes on the bed where she expected him to be.

It was empty.

Was he on the balcony? In the bathroom?

She checked everywhere. Even in the closet, but the room was as empty as she'd left it that morning. Besides the bed being made and the bathroom cleaned spotless, not a single thing appeared to be out of place.

Huh.

She was surprised, and even worse, disappointment tugged at her conscience. Why had he picked now to stop being a pest? When she was finally getting used to having him around? When the idea of spending a little time with him didn't repulse her?

Maybe she was just being impatient. Maybe he was going to give her time to settle in, then he would show up, all prepared to annoy her.

She could wait.

She kicked off her sandals and fluffed her hair with her fingers. Besides the times that it was wet and snarled, today was the first time Dillon had seen her hair down. Not that it looked all that different than it had ten years ago. It was a little longer, but still had a hint of unruly curl to it. Her mom used to nag her incessantly about it.

"Would you please do something with that mop," she would complain when Ivy would let her hair dry loose and wavy. Which she did ninety-nine percent of the time.

Looking back, she remembered her mom nagged her constantly. She still did. About her hair and her clothes and her makeup. Her *posture*. Areas in which she considered herself an authority.

"If you learned to use eyeliner correctly your eyes wouldn't look so small," she would say, or, "I saw you interviewed on CNN and as usual you were slouching. Would it kill you to sit up straight?"

Most people would be proud to have a daughter who even made it on CNN. But her mom didn't see it that way. Nothing was ever good enough for her.

Ivy wondered if her mom had nagged her dad like that. That might have been enough to drive him away. Or maybe he just hadn't been ready for the responsibility of a family. And still wasn't if the rare Christmas card and occasional birthday call were any indication. After years of trying to build some sort of relationship with him, Ivy had come to terms with the fact that it would probably never happen.

She wondered, if she had stayed with Dillon, would the same thing have happened to their children? Would he have been an absentee dad? He'd made it all too clear that he hadn't been ready for children then. Maybe he never would be.

It was one of those subjects that they'd never brought up. One of many.

She glanced over at the digital clock beside the bed. It was eight-fifteen and he still hadn't shown up. How much longer did he plan to make her wait?

Until she was tucked into bed and sleeping?

If that was how he wanted to play this, fine. If he could wait, so could she.

To pass the time she opened her laptop and launched her e-mail program. Might as well do something constructive while she waited.

There were the usual three hundred or so e-mails for male enhancement drugs guaranteeing her a larger penis in six months, erectile dysfunction drugs at a deep discount and replica watches for rock-bottom prices. There was also a message from her writing partner, Miranda Reed, marked Urgent. The body of the e-mail was a series of question marks and exclamation points.

There was a second message that simply said, *call me!* in fifty-point, hot-pink type.

Ivy had promised to call her the instant she learned the identity of the mystery best man. She'd been so far off-kilter, she'd completely forgotten.

She dug her cell phone from her purse, and, sure enough, there were a dozen missed calls and half as many voice messages.

She dialed the number and Miranda answered on the first ring. "Who is he?"

Ivy laughed. "Hello to you, too."

"Have pity. The suspense is killing me. Is he dark and sexy? Does he bear a striking resemblance to Johnny Depp or Antonio Banderas?"

In the weeks before the trip they had speculated who the mystery man might be, coming up with both the best-case scenario—he looked like Johnny or Antonio with a body to die for—or worst case—he would look more like Johnny Cash but older. And he would have a beer gut, thinning hair and ingrown toenails.

In some ways, what she'd ended up with was worse.

"Yes, yes, no, no."

"Okay, dark and sexy is good. Is he nice?"

Rather than play twenty questions, she decided it best to just blurt it out. "He's Dillon."

There was a pause, then, "Like, Matt Dillon?"

"Nope."

"Ugh, not *Bob* Dylan."

"Dillon Marshall."

Another pause while she digested that, then, "You mean, he *looks* like Dillon?"

Oh, didn't she wish. "I mean he *is* Dillon. In the flesh."

"Holy crap."

"Yeah. Surprise." She gave Miranda a blow-by-blow of the trip so far. The way he'd been following her and how they couldn't be together five minutes without arguing. She left out the kissing parts, since they were completely irrelevant, and the way she'd made him jealous today. Oh, and the fact that she actually wanted him to intrude on her. "Deidre thinks I need to let the past go and forgive him."

"Maybe that's good advice."

"Miranda, we can barely say two words to each other without an argument starting. How are we supposed to resolve anything if we can't talk to each other?"

"Maybe you're not trying hard enough."

For a moment she was too stunned to reply. Surely Miranda of all people would be on her side. She would understand what Ivy was going through. Finally she managed a baffled, "Excuse me?"

"Don't take this the wrong way. But you can be stubborn sometimes. Maybe you're just not listening to what he has to say."

"I listen to people for a living. I would not be where I am today if I didn't know how to listen. And you think *I'm* stubborn? You should try having a serious conversation with this man. He's *impossible!*"

Her tone softened. "I swear I'm not saying this to upset you. I'm just worried that the past is holding you back."

"Holding me back how? Is this about my sex life?"

"Well, no, not exactly, although you've got to admit, it *has* been a while."

"Next you're going to tell me that you think I'm unhappy." There was silence at the other end. "You do, don't you? Why is everyone so convinced I'm not happy? I'm a psychologist, for God's sake. Don't you think I would have noticed? If I was so miserable, don't you think I would have done something about it?"

"Maybe you're so used to feeling that way, you don't even realize it's happening. I think…oh, shoot! The other line is ringing." She paused, and Ivy knew she was checking the caller ID. "It's our publicist. We're supposed to make the final arrangements for my trip to New York, for that radio interview. I really should answer."

"That's fine," Ivy said. She'd heard enough, anyway.

"I'll call you right back. I promise."

"I'll talk to you later." Ivy disconnected and shut off her phone. She didn't want to talk to her again. Calling Miranda was supposed to make her feel better, not worse.

If everyone else was so convinced she was miserable, what about Dillon? What did he see when he looked at her? Did he think she was unhappy?

She looked at the clock. It was half-past eight, and she was tired of waiting. If everyone was so darned convinced her unresolved issues with Dillon were ruining her life, then damn it, she was going to resolve them. Once and for all.

Eleven

Self-esteem take a hit? Get past the hurt and move on.
Find a new activity or group to get involved in.
Exercise! Walk! Look in the mirror every day, and
say, "I like that person looking back at me."
—excerpt from *The Modern Woman's Guide to*
Divorce (And the Joy of Staying Single)

Ivy flung open the bedroom door and peered down the length of the hallway. No Dillon. But a narrow sliver of light shone through his partially open door like an written invitation. She marched down the hall, intent on barging in on him before he had the chance to do the same to her.

Rather than knock, since such gestures hadn't been high on his list of priorities, she shoved the door open and stepped right inside.

The first thing she noticed was the binders and loose papers strewn across the bed. The second was Dillon sitting in the middle of it all, back propped against the headboard, reading some official-looking document. He didn't look as though he was preparing to barge in on her anytime soon.

"Problem?" he asked, watching her expectantly.

She just stood there, mouth hanging open, probably looking like a trout stuck on a hook. He was wearing a pair of jogging pants, a Texas A&M T-shirt, and his feet were bare.

He really hadn't been going anywhere. When he said he was going to his room to stay, he'd been telling her the truth. He hadn't been planning to bug her after all.

He set down the papers he'd been reading. "What's wrong? Cat got your tongue?"

She said the first thing that popped into her head, and she said it with…*enthusiasm*. "I am very happy with my life."

He shrugged, looking more than a little confused by her outburst. "Okay."

Now what? Now that she'd just made a complete ass out of herself. "I just wanted you to know that. Because I'm finding out that some people don't think I am."

"Really. Do these people have names?"

"That's not important. The thing is, these people seem to think that my unresolved issues with you are holding me back somehow."

He folded his arms across his chest, looking intrigued now. "Oh, yeah?"

"In case you're wondering, they're not. But, to shut

them up, I'd like us to sit down and talk and figure out what it is that's unresolved, and resolve it. Without arguing or fighting," she added. "In other words, I want us to get along."

"There's only one problem with that," he said. "Your idea of getting along is when I shut my mouth and agree with everything you say."

The accusation stung, and she was about to snap right back at him when she realized that would only start a fight. If they were going to do this she had to be willing to listen to what he had to say, even if it was sarcastic and snotty. Maybe it was the only way he knew to communicate his feelings.

"So what you're saying to me is that you feel I don't listen to you."

He narrowed his eyes at her, as though he wasn't quite sure what to make of that. "Active listening, right?"

The man never ceased to surprise her. "How do you know that?"

"I did go to a few of my classes, you know. And I dated a psychiatrist a couple of years ago."

"Then think how easy this will be."

"For some reason I doubt that," he said. "You sure you want to do this? You want to dredge up the past and try to sort it out after all this time?"

She did and she didn't. All she knew was that Deidre's thinking she was unhappy was an annoyance, but hearing the same thing from Miranda had scared her a little. And though she'd denied it, deep down she couldn't help wondering if they were right. What if they were seeing something she wasn't? What if there was something better out there and she was missing it? What if all this time she'd just been slogging through life, not really living it?

"We at least should try," she said.

"You might not like what I have to say."

She was well aware of that. "I'll take my chances."

"Okay," he agreed. He gathered the papers and tucked them into the binder, then gestured for her to sit.

She perched on the edge at the foot of the bed. "So, where do we start?"

"Since we're new to this communicating thing, maybe we should practice first. Maybe we should try talking about something we never fought about."

That subject did not exist. "Dillon, we fought about *everything*."

"Not everything."

"See, we're fighting already!"

"This is not fighting. This is discussing."

"Name one thing in our entire relationship that we didn't fight about."

"Money," he said.

"Money?"

"Money was never an issue. You nagged me about school and rode me relentlessly about my drinking and my weekend excursions. But never money. Even during the divorce it never came up."

He was right. She may not have approved of the way he spent his money, particularly the trips to Vegas and Atlantic City that would put him back thousands of dollars. But she hadn't felt she had any right to dictate where and how he spent—or wasted—his fortune.

And when the divorce happened, she didn't ask for a penny. She just wanted it to be over fast. And it might have been if his father hadn't gotten involved. Apparently, he hadn't trusted her to fade away quietly. Either that or he was just pissed off that he'd been wrong about her, that she really hadn't been after Dillon's money.

"And sex," he said. "We never fought about sex."

Oh, but they had. One time. It had been *the* argument. The one that had hammered the final wedge between them.

"The day I told you I thought I might be pregnant, we argued. Sex…pregnant. Can't have one without the other."

"And I've been trying for the first one for days now, but you're not cooperating."

Clearly, he used humor as a defense mechanism when she came close to hitting a nerve, to making him face something he didn't want to deal with.

"Don't do that," she said. "Don't make a joke out of this or nothing will get resolved. Just talk to me. I know you're not used to talking about your feelings, but you're going to have to if we really want this to work."

He was quiet for a second and she could see the wheels spinning, see him working things through, trying to decide if this was worth the hassle.

What would it be?

"I had every reason to be upset," he finally said. "Neither of us was ready to start a family."

"You were more than upset." He had been furious.

How could she let that happen, he'd shouted? How could she be so careless? As if he'd had no part in it.

The pregnancy test she later took had been negative, but by then the damage had already been done.

After that it had been as if they were afraid to touch each other, afraid there might be an accident that would bind them together for life. And without the sex, there had been nothing left to hold them together. She knew that it was only a matter of time before everything fell apart. But admitting it was over was as good as admitting that her mom was right. So she had hung on until the bitter end.

"I overreacted," he admitted, then he really blew her away by adding, "I think that deep down I knew I was a lousy husband and thought I would be an even worse father."

It was the most honest thing she had ever heard him say. The first time he'd ever admitted he wasn't flawless, that he had doubts just like everyone else.

"You weren't a lousy husband."

He got that stubborn, sulky look. "You sure as hell made me feel like I was."

Her first instinct was to lash out and deny the accusation. But Dillon was not the kind of man to admit to having feelings he didn't really have. He was too damned proud.

"I didn't mean to," she said.

"It wasn't always that way. After we got married, you changed."

Another denial sat on the tip of her tongue. Why was this so hard? Why was her gut reaction to go on the defensive?

Instead, she asked, "How did I change?"

He shrugged. "You were just…different."

Well, that wasn't much help.

She tried another angle. "What was I like before we got married?"

He thought about it a second, and the hint of a smile pulled at the corners of his mouth. "Fun. You were a little repressed at first, but you were willing to try new things."

They did have fun. So much that she used to believe it was too good to be true. She wondered why a rich, handsome man was even remotely interested in someone as boring and plain as her. Dillon had brought her out of her shell. He'd made her feel good about herself. At least for a while.

The next question was harder to ask, since she was pretty sure she wouldn't like the answer. "And after? What was I like then?"

"You were so…*serious*. All you did was study."

That was entirely unfair. Not everyone had the luxury of screwing around. "I didn't have an eight-figure trust fund to fall back on and a ready-made job being handed to me. I needed to get my degree. And I had to maintain my GPA or I would lose my scholarship. Which, as you know, I eventually lost anyway."

"Because of my father," he said.

She nodded. He'd pulled a few strings and her full scholarship had mysteriously been revoked. She'd worked hard for that money. She'd busted her butt all through high school and graduated at the top of her class.

With the snap of his fingers, Dillon's father had snatched it away. To this day she wasn't exactly sure why.

Was it because she'd never been impressed by his money and power? Because she couldn't be bought? Not for any price.

Maybe he'd done it to put her in her place. To prove the power he held over her.

To add insult to injury, no one would give her a student loan, not when she was married to a billionaire. She'd had to go to work full-time to cover her tuition and living expenses until the divorce was final, and Dillon's father saw to it that it took a very *long* time. By then she was so far behind, she'd graduated two years later than she'd originally planned.

"I didn't find out what he'd done until it was too late," Dillon said. "If I had known at the time I would have stopped him. Or at least I would have tried."

She'd convinced herself that he'd known all along and had let it happen, and she'd hated him for it. But the truth was, he'd never been vindictive. Just arrogant and misguided.

And she believed him. If he could have stopped it, he would have.

"Working harder for it just made me appreciate it more," she told him, and it was the truth. It taught her to be independent and self-sufficient. She learned she was tough enough to handle just about anything.

"I would have paid your tuition if you had only asked."

She knew that, too, but she'd been too proud to go looking for a handout. Too embarrassed to admit how badly she had screwed up. She had to do it on her own. As Miranda had said earlier, Ivy had a stubborn streak.

"You didn't even have to go to school," he told her. "I would have taken care of you."

"I'm sure my dad said the same thing to my mom. Then he walked out the door. Besides, if I had quit school, we both would have been bored silly within a month."

"Probably," he agreed.

"So, I guess our marriage failed because I was a good student," she said, half joking. He didn't return her smile.

"It wasn't just that."

Oh, great, there was more? Was there anything she did right?

"You sure you want to hear this?"

She wasn't sure of anything anymore. "No, but tell me anyway."

"After we got married you nagged me constantly."

Oh, *ouch*. That one really stung.

Her mother's nagging had driven her nuts. Had she really done the same thing to Dillon? "I nagged you?"

"No matter what I did, it wasn't good enough."

That wasn't true. Although she did recall thinking that being married hadn't been what she'd expected. In fact, it hadn't been any different than when they'd been dating. Dillon hadn't changed at all.

Maybe *that* had been the problem. She'd been expecting him to change. To mature overnight.

"I think I had certain expectations about being married," she told him. "I thought we would settle down and get serious. Start acting like grown-ups. But things didn't happen the way I planned. You were so…irresponsible. I think maybe it scared me."

"I wasn't ready to grow up," he said. No apology, no excuses. Hadn't that always been his M.O.? This is the way things are and if you don't like it, tough cookies. But that wasn't the way it worked.

"Part of marriage is learning to compromise," she reminded him.

He opened his mouth to argue, she could see it in his

eyes. That stubborn, I'm-right-and-you're-wrong look. Then he caught himself.

Jeez, were they both that stubborn?

He sighed and rested his head back against the headboard. "You're right. It is. I guess maybe I felt as though you were asking me to be something I wasn't."

"And the harder I pushed you to change, the more you rebelled and acted the complete opposite."

He nodded. "Yeah, I guess so."

"And the more you rebelled, the harder I nagged and pushed, making things even worse."

"Until we self-destructed."

"Exactly."

And there it was. Their entire relationship in a nutshell. It was a genuine "lightbulb" moment.

Two stubborn people, neither willing to meet the other halfway. She had never considered the possibility that it wasn't entirely his fault. It had never even crossed her mind.

"All this time I've had myself convinced that it had to be either your fault or mine. But the truth is, we both screwed up. It's both our faults, isn't it?"

"I guess so."

"We were young and stupid and had no clue what we were getting ourselves into."

He shook his head. "Well, damn. I guess I'm not as perfect as I thought I was."

Neither of them were.

Knowing that, accepting it, seemed to lift the weight of the past ten years from her shoulders. She felt free.

Until the meaning of it, the repercussions, dropped

on her like a ten-ton block of solid steel. Then she just felt like she wanted to barf.

She'd been basing her life's work on her own experiences, her own failed marriage. All this time she held herself up on some sort of pedestal. She'd been wronged, she was the victim. The real truth was, she had been just as responsible.

She was a statistic. Just like everyone else.

Even worse, she was a fraud.

Half of what she'd written in her book had turned out to be untrue, and the other half was skewed so far out of proportion it was hardly credible.

How many times, as a form of therapy, had she suggested her patients write down their feelings in a personal journal, or in a letter that they would later shred? To accept and validate their emotions. Which is exactly what she'd done. Then she'd sent them off to a publisher and printed them for the whole world to see.

And the really frightening part was people had actually listened. They had taken the ranting of a hurt, embittered woman and made them sacred.

What had she done?

And how could she justify doing it again?

She had a contract. She'd taken an advance. It was too late to back out now. To say, oops, I was wrong. What I said before, just ignore that. *This* is what you should really do.

She didn't even know what *this* was. What if she never figured it out?

"You look disturbed," Dillon said, genuine concern in his eyes. "I thought you would be happy."

"I am," she lied, because to admit what she was really feeling was a humiliation she just couldn't bear. And she owed him a *huge* apology. "I'm sorry for all those things I wrote about you."

He shrugged. "Like you said, you didn't write a single thing that wasn't true."

"Maybe, but I had no right to publish it in a book. If I had issues about our marriage, the only person I should have talked to was you or my shrink."

"I guess we've both made our share of mistakes. What do you say we forget what happened in the past and start fresh. Right here, right now."

He had every right to hold what she'd done against her. Instead, he was willing to forgive and forget. And she would be wise to do the same. "I'd like that."

He looked at her for a second, just looked at her face, as if he were seeing it for the first time. She wondered what he saw. If he could tell how conflicted she felt.

"You want to get out of here?" he asked.

"And go where?"

He shrugged. "Does it matter?"

He was right, it didn't matter. As long as she was anywhere but here, torturing herself.

She couldn't run from the past any longer, and she couldn't change the fact that her life was in total chaos. But this was a vacation, darn it.

She would worry about fixing this mess after the wedding. Tonight, she just wanted to forget.

Twelve

It can be very tempting, particularly on lonely nights, to look up your ex. But the more you fall back on your old ways, the harder it will be to truly move on.
—excerpt from *The Modern Woman's Guide to Divorce (And the Joy of Staying Single)*

It began as a walk on the beach. The air was warm and a full moon hung low in the sky, lighting their way. They didn't say much. Just strolled quietly side by side. Then Dillon suggested they walk to the village for a drink, and alcohol in any form sounded pretty good to her.

When they got there they found themselves in the middle of a Mexican carnival. Colorful lanterns and twinkling lights lined the street, and the air was scented with a mouthwatering combination of sugar and spicy fried food.

They snacked on authentic Mexican treats, drank salty margaritas and danced to a live salsa band. The evening was a blur of bodies, bumping and grinding, laughter and fun. Ivy couldn't remember the last time she'd felt more relaxed and...*alive*. Hadn't it always been that way with Dillon? The man excelled at having a good time.

It was well after midnight when they headed back to the villa. They were halfway there before she realized Dillon was holding her hand. She'd obviously been impaired by the alcohol, because she liked the way it felt. She didn't pull away. Not even when they went inside. If someone saw them that way, they could get the wrong idea. Or maybe it was the right idea. Either way it could get very messy and complicated for both of them. But mostly for her.

It wasn't fair. It wasn't right that after everything they had been through, after all the pain he'd caused her, Ivy still wanted him this much. Of all the possible men in the world, why did it have to be him? Why did he have to be the one?

It was dark and still in the villa. Probably everyone else was already in bed. As he walked her up the stairs, disappointment began to tug at her insides.

She didn't want this night to end. She wanted to make this last, to feel happy just a little while longer. She didn't want to fall asleep and wake knowing that it wouldn't happen again.

She wanted to invite him into her room. She wanted

him naked in her bed. One last time before they said goodbye forever.

That was a terrible idea. She should be trying to figure things out, not make them worse. And being caught sleeping with her ex would definitely make things worse.

Ivy would never hear the end of it from her mother. There was nothing she loved more than reminding Ivy of the mistakes she'd made, and finding new ones to nag her about.

So the decision that suited her best interest was to say good-night and go to sleep.

When they reached her bedroom door, she turned to him. To tell him she'd had a good time, and she was glad they could part from this vacation on better terms. Heck, maybe they could even be friends. But before she knew what was happening, Dillon was kissing her. And even worse, she was kissing him back. Not just your run-of-the-mill making out, either. They were ravaging each other, as if they were battling over who wanted it more.

His mouth still on hers, he backed her into the room and shut the door. She couldn't comprehend much over the moans and breathless sounds she had begun making, but she was pretty sure she heard the lock turn. Then Dillon was walking her backward. She wasn't sure where until the backs of her thighs collided with the mattress.

She was vaguely aware that she was pulling at his clothes. She wanted skin. Didn't matter where. Just something to put her hands on. She *needed* to put her hands on him.

Before she could get his shirt pulled from the waist

of his slacks, she was on her back lying sideways across the bed, her calves dangling over the edge. And she couldn't touch Dillon because he had her wrists pinned over her head with one of his hands.

Then he was kissing her, pushing her clothes out of the way so he had more area to explore. More to touch. Her stomach, her rib cage, and…oh! Her breasts. First through her bra, then he pushed that out of the way, too. Somewhere in the back of her mind she was thinking how small she was there, how he must have had much better, much bigger. Then she felt his mouth, hot and wet, and as long as he kept touching her, just like that, she didn't care what size they were.

She felt his hand on her thigh and the sensation was so foreign to her, so exquisitely intense, she gasped and jerked with surprise.

Dillon stopped what he was doing and looked at her, his lids heavy. "Do you want me to stop?"

Oddly enough, his asking was even worse than if he were to ravage her without her permission. If she didn't take this opportunity to stop him, she would only have herself to blame. And at the same time, she couldn't stop herself from thinking it would be worth every bit of grief it caused her.

"Yes or no?" he asked, his eyes dark and intense. And she had no doubt that if she told him no, he would stop. No questions asked.

"Don't stop."

A hungry smile curled his mouth and the hand on her thigh began to slide upward.

At that point she knew there was no turning back. It was a done deal. She was going to sleep with Dillon. She was going to have sex with her ex-husband.

She really was crazy.

His breath was hot on her skin as he nibbled and kissed his way down her body. Touching, tasting. His fingers slipped inside the leg of her shorts, brushing against her panties…

At that point things began to get fuzzy. One minute her shorts were on, the next they had mysteriously disappeared. The same thing happened to her panties. Then Dillon was touching her. Slow, steady pressure. Warm and slippery.

She closed her eyes and gave herself permission to relax and enjoy. How could she have thought she didn't need this? How had she gone so long without a man's touch?

And no man knew her body the way Dillon did. No one made her feel as good. And what the hell was wrong with feeling good every now and then? Who better than a man who needed no road map to please her, who would never expect or want more than a very brief physical relationship? A fling.

Without warning Dillon pressed her thighs open, lowered his head and took her into his mouth. The sensation was so wickedly intense she cried out. Her hands fisted in his hair and she was making sounds, raspy and nonsensical. She didn't seem to have any control left. She was flying on autopilot, and about to crash and burn.

Her breath was coming hard and fast, and the room

slipped in and out of focus. Each individual sensation merged and tangled and fused together like the wick on a stick of dynamite, then it sparked and ignited.

The flame hissed and licked its way up, building and climbing. And when it reached her core, she blew apart, splintered into a million pieces.

She hovered there, somewhere between pain and pleasure, conscious and unconscious.

It seemed as though she melted back together, one little piece at a time, slowly, gradually, her pulse returning to normal. When she finally opened her eyes, Dillon was there, leaning over her. Watching. Waiting for her to return from the outer stratosphere. Then he leaned down and kissed her. So gently, *so* sweetly.

"I'll see you later, Ivy."

Wait. What?

Later?

She sat up, still dizzy and a little disoriented. "Where are you going?"

"My room."

"But…" They had just gotten started.

"I don't understand," she said. "Did I do something wrong?"

He looked almost…sad. Which made no sense at all. "No. You did everything right."

"Then why are you leaving?"

"You know where I'll be if you need me."

Then he left, closing the door quietly behind him. For several minutes she was too stunned to process what had just happened. To make sense of it.

Was this just another part of the game for him?

Wasn't it enough that she'd let him into her room? That she'd let him touch her?

Apparently not.

What did he want? For her to chase him? Would he settle for nothing less than total surrender?

And wasn't that just like him?

She didn't know if she should feel angry or hurt or disappointed, so she allowed herself all three. Was he honestly that arrogant? He had chased her relentlessly for days; now he was just going to turn his back on her?

Unless…

Maybe Dillon wasn't as sure of himself, as self-confident, as she'd assumed. Maybe he needed her to come to him. Maybe, like her, he'd spent so long pushing people away, he had no idea how to let someone back inside.

Was it possible that under that arrogant facade he was just as lost and confused as she was?

And lonely.

Very, very lonely.

The idea was as sad as it was empowering.

And she knew exactly what she needed to do.

Ivy stepped into Dillon's room. The light beside the bed was on, but he wasn't lying there.

Her eyes were drawn to the curtains blowing in the open French doors. Dillon stood on the balcony, his back to her, leaning on the edge. He wore nothing but a pair of loose silk pajama bottoms.

She walked up behind him, and though she didn't make a sound, he sensed her there.

"You lost?" he asked, not turning around.

Lost?

She'd been lost for the last ten years and was only now beginning to realize it.

"No," she told him, hearing a quiver in her voice. Everything about him, about being close to him, both frightened and excited her. "For the first time in a long time I know exactly where I am."

He just stood there, facing the ocean. She knew what he was waiting for. He wanted her to make the first move. He needed that validation.

The idea gave her an unfamiliar but exhilarating sense of power.

She stepped up behind him and lightly touched his bare back. He didn't tense, didn't flinch, as though he'd been expecting it. She flattened her hands, smoothed her palms across warm skin, feeling only lean muscle underneath. His back rose and fell steadily as he breathed, while her own breath seemed to be coming faster. She could feel the steady beat of his pulse while her own fluctuated wildly, knocking around inside of her chest like a Mexican jumping bean.

She slipped her hands around to rest over his solid abdomen just above his waistband, and felt the muscles contract. She pressed her cheek to his back, breathed in the scent of his skin, felt that rush of familiarity pour over her.

His hands didn't stray from their perch on the railing but he said, "You're trembling."

"I'm scared," she admitted and she let her hands wander higher, across his chest.

"No reason to be scared."

She had every reason to be scared, to be terrified, even.

She was falling for him again. She was falling for a man she knew she could never have. They were stuck in a hopeless situation. A vicious cycle of piss-poor timing.

But she'd come too far to stop now. She was going through with this. She'd never wanted anything more.

She undid the tie on her robe and let it fall to the balcony floor, then pressed the length of her naked body against him. He sucked in a breath and groaned somewhere deep inside. She could feel it rumble through him, through muscle and skin into her breasts and her fingers and the curve of her belly.

They stood that way for several minutes, neither moving or making a sound. It was…nice, but she wasn't looking for nice. She wanted fantastic. She wanted mind-blowing, rip-roaring ecstasy.

She dragged her nails lightly down his chest, from his shoulders all the way to his waistband, felt him tense. He was trying to be strong, trying to milk this for all he could but she could feel him losing it. And she liked it. She liked being the one in control.

She continued her exploration downward, just below his silky waistband, teased him there. "You told me you don't wear pajamas."

His reply came out breathy and uneven. "I lied."

"I know you want me. Are you going to make me beg?"

She could swear she felt him smile. "That's not a problem, is it?"

He turned abruptly, and before she knew it she was in his arms. Body to body, soul to soul. Then he was kissing her. And, oh, did he know how to kiss. He took control, possessed *her*. If he had wanted her to be the aggressor in this scenario, that moment had passed.

And what gave him the right? What if she wanted to be the one calling the shots for a change?

His hands wandered down her back, over her behind, his erection long and hard between them behind the slippery silk. He cupped her backside and squeezed so she bit his lip. Hard.

He gasped and jerked and for a second she thought she'd gone too far.

"Did I hurt you?"

His lids were heavy, eyes glassy and unfocused as he gazed down at her. "Yeah, but I liked it."

So she did it again. She wrapped her hands around his head, pulled him down for a kiss, and sank her teeth into his lower lip. Dillon groaned and tunneled his fingers through her hair, fisted his hands in it. He pulled her head back to look at her, hovering on the line between pain and pleasure. This time there was a smile on his face. "I'm not sure what happened to you in the past ten years, but I like it."

"It gets better." She reached into his pajama bottoms and circled a hand around his erection. He mumbled a curse and his eyes rolled up. But when she tried to pull the pajamas down she only got them halfway past his hips before he caught her hand.

"We're outside," he reminded her.

She knew that. And to top it all off the light from the bedroom was silhouetting their bodies quite clearly.

"Oh, yeah?" She shook off his hand and shoved his pajamas the rest of the way down. "What's your point?"

Then she was off her feet. She gasped as her back slammed hard against the villa wall beside the door. She was pinned between the door and the balcony railing, between rough stucco and Dillon's long, lean body. He hesitated for a second, went stone still, as though he was afraid *he* might have gone too far.

"Did I hurt you?" he asked.

She wrapped her legs around his hips and ground herself against him, so he could feel how wet she was. "Yeah, but I liked it."

He seemed to know exactly what she wanted, and he didn't hesitate. He drove himself inside her, hard and swift and so deep that she cried out. With pain and shock and pure ecstasy.

Dillon pulled out, hovered there for a second, torturing her. Then he plunged forward, and she gasped as the rough wall dug into her back. She'd spent such a long time dulling her feelings, pretending they didn't matter. Now all she wanted to do was feel. Pleasure and lust and pain. She wanted it all, right here, right now. There was no such thing as too much.

"Harder," she gasped and he drove hard against her, inside her. And when it wasn't hard enough, she dug her nails into his back, dragged them across his skin. *"Harder."*

He did as she asked. He may have been the one driving, but she had her foot on the accelerator. She was still in control.

She could feel him tensing, feel him losing it. Bit by bit.

She was doing that to him. *She* was making him lose control.

And when he took the plunge, when he shuddered and roared with release, she went over with him.

Thirteen

Nothing will change for you until you take control of your life and decide that you will be happy. You need movement in a positive forward direction.
—excerpt from *The Modern Woman's Guide to Divorce (And the Joy of Staying Single)*

There were orgasms, and then there were *orgasms*. The kind that grabbed hold and didn't let go until the absolute last bit of energy had been wrenched out. The kind that released so many endorphins and pheromones that it took several minutes for her body to realize it was twisted like a pretzel, to register that the tingling in her back was not from arousal, but the sharp stucco facade shredding her skin like cheddar on a cheese grater.

"Ow."

Dillon lifted his head from her shoulder, where he'd dropped it a few minutes ago while he caught his breath. He shifted and she winced. "Problem?"

"Wall...sharp."

Only then did she notice the grimace on his face. "Disengage your claws and I'll let you down."

Oh, jeez! She hadn't even realized she was still clinging to him. She loosened her grip and he eased her away from the wall and set her on her feet.

He pulled her into the bedroom, into the light. "Turn around. Let me see the damage."

He examined her back and she watched him over her shoulder, trying to gauge his expression. "How bad is it?"

"Is the dress you're wearing for the wedding backless by any chance?"

"Yeah, why?"

"Then it's bad."

"How bad?"

"It looks like someone ran a belt sander across your back. And you have pieces of the wall still stuck to your skin."

"That would explain the pain, I guess."

He touched her lightly between her shoulder blades and the sting made her wince. "We need to get this cleaned up."

He turned her again and nudged her in the direction of the bathroom. When they were inside he switched on the light. Just like her bathroom, it was really bright with lots of mirror space. Miles of it. The floor-to-ceiling kind that screamed out each and every detail, down to the tiniest imperfection. Ivy crossed her arms over her breasts and sucked in her tummy, wishing she could suck in her hips, too. And her butt.

Dillon had no imperfections, she noticed, as he rummaged through his shaving kit. Nope. He looked just fine. Nicely shaped butt, muscular thighs...

He turned and crouched down to check the cupboard under the sink. She had to slap a hand over her mouth to keep from gasping in horror.

He emerged with a first aid kit, and when he saw the look on her face asked, "What's wrong?"

"Your tuxedo isn't backless, is it?"

He turned to the mirror, inspecting the long red welts criss-crossing his back from his shoulders all the way down to his butt. "I never knew you had such a wild side."

She bit her lip. "Sorry."

He hooked a hand behind her neck, drew her to him and kissed her. Not quite passionate, but not a peck, either. "Darlin', that was not a complaint."

He let her go and set the first aid kit on the bathroom counter. He rummaged through it for cotton and antiseptic. How could he be so casual? Didn't he feel the least bit self-conscious standing there naked? She sure did.

"Turn around." He dabbed antiseptic on the cotton. "This might sting."

When the cool liquid touched her raw skin she tensed and sucked in a breath.

"Sorry." He dabbed slowly and gently, starting at the top and working his way down. She wondered what he was thinking. If he was looking at her and noticing the way her body had...*spread.*

"My body has changed," she said, in case he hadn't

noticed. So he wouldn't suddenly look at her and think *Ack, who is this cow I've been sleeping with?* "I don't look like I did in college."

"Good," he said, looking at her in the mirror. "I'm turned on by women, not girls."

Oh, well, lucky her.

He tossed the used cotton in the trash and fished out a fresh one. "Besides, you don't really look all that different."

"I think your memory is failing."

"My memory is crystal clear," he said, flashing a devious grin over her shoulder. "I have video."

Video? "What kind of video?"

"*The* video," he said.

Her jaw dropped and her heart bottomed out. She hadn't thought about *the* video for years. She had no reason to, considering he'd told her he erased it.

"Our *special* video?" she asked. "The one you absolutely *swore* you got rid of?"

"I lied."

There were things on that video that she'd done for him, done to herself, without him in the frame, that he could have at any time used against her. He could have ruined her career. Her *life!*

"All done." He tossed the used cotton in the trash and turned her toward him.

"Why did you keep it?"

"I wasn't planning on using it against you, if that's what you're thinking. We made that for us. No one else is going to see it. *Ever.*"

Well, that was good to know. And it made her feel

like even more of a slime for the things she'd written in her book. How could she have been so vindictive and immature? He'd had the ammunition to retaliate big-time, but he hadn't done it.

"I am such an ass," she said.

He sat on the edge of the counter and pulled her closer, between his slightly parted knees. God, he was beautiful. And she must be completely nuts, totally off her rocker to be standing here naked with him, casually chatting, as though they hadn't just had sex so wild and out of control that they'd required first aid afterward.

And it would be a lie if she said she didn't want to do it again.

"Are you angry?" he asked.

She wasn't sure what to feel.

He pried her arms from their position guarding her chest and took her hands in his, weaving his fingers through hers. "The truth is, I don't really know why I kept it. I didn't even remember I had it until about a week ago. It was stashed in the back of my safe."

A ripple of excitement, a shiver of anticipation, rippled across her skin. "Did you…watch it?"

He nodded.

Oh. My. God.

Just talking about it was getting him hard again. Not just getting. He was already there. And she was feeling that warm, fuzzy sensation. It started in her scalp and worked its way south toward her toes in a slow, easy rush.

She could hardly believe what she was going to ask next. Something was definitely wrong with her. "Then what did you do?"

A grin quirked up the corner of his mouth. "Are you sure you want to know?"

She did and she didn't. But mostly she did, despite the fact that it was a little depraved and incredibly kinky.

She nodded.

"I watched it…" He rounded his hands over her hips, pulled her a little closer. "Then I went up to my room…" He leaned forward and nibbled her neck, her shoulder. "I took off my clothes…" His breath was warm on her ear and Ivy felt hot and cold all over—

"Then I took a very long, cold shower."

Embarrassment burned her cheeks. She buried her face in the crook of his shoulder. "That was mean."

He laughed. "I had you going, though."

She took a moment to breathe in his scent, to enjoy the way their bodies fit together, every dip and curve. It felt exactly the same. It felt…*right*.

And *so* wrong.

"What are we doing, Dillon?" She looked up at him. "We're divorced."

"Last I heard there's no law against sleeping with your ex." He tucked her hair back behind her ears. It was such a simple, sweet gesture of affection. One you did after being with someone for a long time. And that was kind of what this felt like. As though they hadn't really been apart for ten long years. It was as if it had been a week or two and they were picking up exactly where they'd left off.

Only wiser.

"How's your back feel?"

Back? What back? With his arms wrapped around

her, his body warm and close, she hadn't even noticed. "It feels much better."

"I guess we got a little carried away."

"I guess we did."

"I pride myself on my stamina, but you took me down in seconds flat," he admitted. "Before tonight, no one has ever managed to do that."

"Is that a fact?" She took his hands and pulled him backward toward the door. "Well, then, maybe we oughtta' go into the bedroom and see if I can do that again."

It mystified Ivy how some things never changed. She and Dillon had fallen easily back into their old routine. They made love, talked for a while, then made love again. Repeating the cycle until the hazy light of dawn crept up on them.

It was as frightening as it was settling. To know someone so well, but not really know them at all. To realize that as good as it could be, they had nowhere to take this. No future.

They lay curled up in the dark under the covers facing each other, arms and legs entwined, as though they couldn't bear the idea of not touching each other. Not being close. Not looking each other in the eye.

Maybe because they both knew that after this week it might never happen again.

"Why didn't you ever remarry?" she asked him.

He shrugged. "I guess once was enough. How about you?"

"I guess I never met anyone I liked enough to make that kind of commitment."

"You always were a little commitment phobic," he said, but she could tell by his smile he was teasing. "How many times did I have to ask you out before you finally said yes?"

"Enough that I realized you weren't ever going to stop asking. I was so nervous on that first date. I was so afraid you were going to try to take advantage of me. But you were a perfect gentleman."

"And it nearly killed me. The way I wanted you." He smiled and shook his head. "That was the longest three months of my entire life."

"I never told you this, but you were my first."

"Yeah, I sorta figured."

"You never said anything."

"I thought that if you wanted me to know you would have said so."

"Right from the start we didn't talk to each other, did we? We couldn't be honest. Maybe we just didn't know how."

"I guess we finally figured it out," he said.

"Yeah, ten years too late."

"Is it?"

"Is it what?"

"Too late."

He couldn't be serious. She propped herself up on her elbow. "You know that after this week, this has to end. It can't go any further than this bedroom. If it were to get out, that would be the end of my career. My writing, my practice. I would lose everything."

He sighed and rolled onto his back. "I guess that is a lot to ask, isn't it?"

"Besides, my mom would disown me if you and I ever got back together."

He grinned. "She never did like me much."

"And how would your mother react if you brought me home for dinner?"

"I'm thinking...stroke, heart attack."

She scooted up close to him and rested her head on his chest, sighed as his arms went around her. She had gone far too long without this. When she got back to the States, she would have to start dating again. Start living her life instead of watching it roll past without her. "We have until Sunday. Three more days. Let's just enjoy them while we can."

"Sounds like a plan."

It was a *good* plan, so why couldn't she shake the feeling, the fear, that three days with Dillon wouldn't be nearly enough?

A loud, insistent pounding roused Ivy from a dead sleep. She tried to open her eyes but the room was too bright.

What time was it?

She squinted at the clock. They'd been sleeping for a whole three and a half hours.

The pounding stopped, then immediately started up again. Beside her, Dillon groaned and stuffed the pillow over his head.

She gave him a poke. "Someone is knocking on your door."

"No kidding," he said, his voice muffled and cranky. He never had been a morning person. Of course, they

hadn't gone to sleep until after seven, so this was tech-
nically like the middle of the night. "They'll go away."

They didn't. Whoever it was pounded harder, then
Dale called, "Dillon, wake up! It's important!"

Dillon mumbled and cursed. He flung the covers off
and rolled out of bed, naked and beautiful. She couldn't
have asked for a better view. A full moon in the morning.

She watched as he grabbed his robe and shoved his
arms through the sleeves, then stomped to the door. He
flung it open and in his cranky voice asked, *"What?"*

"Have you seen Blake and Deidre?"

"Of course not. I was sound asleep."

"Well, they're not here," Dale said. "No one knows
where they are."

"And you think they're in here with me? You picked a
hell of a time to pretend you give a shit about your brother.
They probably went out to breakfast or something."

"I don't think so. They left yesterday afternoon, and
they haven't been back."

Ivy sat up in bed, instantly awake.

"Are you sure they haven't been here?" Dillon asked.
The crankiness was gone and concern had crept in to
take its place.

"The rental car was gone all night and their bed
wasn't slept in."

Fear lodged in Ivy's gut. Deidre had been in pretty
bad shape the other night. Ivy should have checked on
her yesterday. She should have made sure she was okay.

What if she'd had another meltdown? What if she
was in a hospital somewhere?

"I thought Ivy might know where they are," Dale said, "but I can't find her, either."

"I haven't seen her," Dillon lied.

Something was definitely not right. Deidre wouldn't just take off. Not without telling someone.

Ivy wrapped herself in the sheet and joined Dillon at the door. "Did you try calling her cell?"

It was almost funny the way Dale's mouth fell open, how he looked from her, to Dillon, then back to her.

"Oh, there you are, Ivy," Dillon said, acting surprised to see her. "How did you get in here?"

She shot him a look, then turned to Dale. "Did you call their cell phones? Deidre always keeps hers on and charged. She's fanatical about it."

"I tried calling them both and the calls go straight to voice mail."

"Did you try calling your parents?" Dillon asked.

He shook his head. "I didn't want to worry them."

"Something isn't right," Ivy said.

"You know my brother. With our parents flying in tonight, there's no way Blake would just take off."

"Give us five minutes to get dressed," Dillon said. "Then we'll figure out what to do."

"The only thing left to do is call the police," Dillon told everyone an hour and a half later.

They had called everyone they could think of who might possibly know where Deidre and Blake went. Friends, family, coworkers. They called the local hospital to see if anyone matching their descriptions had been admitted, and checked CNN just in case any accidents or unidentified tourists had been found. They had covered all the bases, and they had come up with nothing.

Deidre and Blake were gone.

"We shouldn't be so quick to jump to conclusions," one of the Tweedles said. Dillon still couldn't tell them apart.

"Yeah," the other one added. "I'm sure they're fine."

Everyone else was worried, while those two had done nothing but sulk. Probably because the attention was no longer focused on them.

Ivy was handling it the worst. She couldn't sit still. Dillon would convince her to sit down and relax, and she would be back up again in a minute or two, peering out the window for a sign of their car. Checking her cell phone for a missed call, even though it hadn't once left her hand.

"We should make the call," Dale said, and Calvin nodded in agreement.

Dillon flipped open his phone and was getting ready to dial when they heard a car coming up the driveway.

Ivy dashed to the window. "They're back!"

Relief hit Dillon hard and swift, like a sucker punch in the gut. He snapped his phone shut and slipped it back into the holster. Blake had better have had a damned good excuse for scaring them all half to death.

Tweedle number one followed Ivy to the window and peered out. "See, I told you they were fine."

Ivy turned and shot her a look. One that would have scared Dillon had he been on the receiving end.

"She's got a lot of nerve just taking off," number two said indignantly. "Does she think *we* actually want to be here?"

No, Dillon thought, they had made it pretty clear they were there under duress.

Ivy didn't say a word, but he could see her temper rising. Her cheeks were getting red and blotchy and her fists were clenching and unclenching. And her foot was tapping. Bad sign. If those two knew what was good for them they would quit while they were ahead. Especially with Ivy standing within swinging distance. He knew from experience that you could only push her so far before she blew, and she looked as though she was more than halfway there already.

"Enough, Heather," Dale said.

They actually had names. Go figure. And he was getting kind of attached to Dum and Dee.

"Why are you getting mad at me?" Heather snapped back. "I'm not the one with the problem. You should have seen the way she flipped out the other night."

"Yeah," number one agreed. "It's not our fault that she's too fat to fit in her dress."

The last word had barely left her mouth and Ivy was already in midswing. Dillon scarcely had time to cringe before she connected. One quick, solid right jab, and Tweedle number one was on the ground, holding her jaw.

Everyone else stood in stunned silence. Even number two, aka Heather, didn't seem to know what to say. Or maybe she just didn't want to be the next one to go down.

Then the door flew open and Deidre burst through, Blake close behind. "Hi, everyone! We're back!"

Fourteen

Is the new man in your life pressing for a commitment? Consider wisely. When it comes to relationships, three out of four women make the same mistake twice.
—excerpt from *The Modern Woman's Guide to Divorce (And the Joy of Staying Single)*

They had *eloped.*

Apparently, the dress incident had been the last straw. When Deidre pulled herself together she'd told Blake that if they didn't get out of there, if he didn't make some serious changes, the wedding was off. And thank goodness Blake was smart enough to know what he would have been giving up if he'd let her go.

If Ivy didn't love Deidre so much, she would kill her

for scaring them. But put in the same position, she wouldn't have done things any differently. At least she knew everything was going to be okay. Deidre and Blake would make it. They would be happy.

Now, if only she could feel so confident about her own life.

"You couldn't wait until I got inside the house," Deidre said, handing Ivy a new bag of ice and taking the melted one. "You had to take her down right *before* I walked in."

Ivy set the ice over her swollen, purple knuckles. "It's not as though I planned to hit her. It just sort of happened."

She barely even remembered doing it. One minute she was just standing there, the next Dum was on the floor and Ivy's hand was throbbing. She'd never hit another person in her life. There had just been the beer bottle incident, and luckily for them both she had missed.

When Dee recovered from the shock, she'd begun to wail about calling her attorney and pressing charges, then the four of them had packed up and left. The villa had been blessedly peaceful ever since.

"How's the hand, Sugar Ray?" Dillon asked. He sat in a chair across from Ivy, a goofy grin plastered on his face. He was enjoying this far too much.

"I think I'm going to cut my boxing career short."

"It looks as though you two are getting along better," Deidre said, looking back and forth between them.

"I guess you could say we're working things out," Ivy told her.

"I'm glad. At least this trip wasn't a total waste."

"Have you told Blake's parents?"

"We called them from the road and caught them just as they were leaving for the airport."

"I'm a disgrace to my family," Blake said. "And I'm probably out of a job. And a house."

"And you guys are okay with that?" Ivy asked.

He shrugged and sat on the arm of the couch, beside his new wife. She smiled up at him. "They'll get over it."

"Do you have anything lined up?" Dillon asked him.

"Not yet," Blake said.

"I've said it before and I'll say it again. If you need a job, there's always a position open for you in my company."

"I'll definitely think about it." He looked down at Deidre and grinned. "Right now I just want to enjoy being a newlywed."

"We've decided to leave early for our honeymoon," Deidre told them. "We're going to drive up the coast, then be back in time for the cruise when it leaves Saturday night. Either of you is welcome to stay for the rest of the week." She shot Ivy a smile. "Or both of you."

Ivy struggled to suppress the depraved excitement clawing its way to the surface. She glanced over at Dillon and saw that he was trying really hard not to smile. She didn't doubt they were thinking the exact same thing.

Three days alone, with this big house all to themselves.

Did it get any better than that?

Sunday came way too soon.

After spending every waking hour together for the past three days, the idea of being apart was almost impossible for Dillon to fathom.

As he helped her carry her bags out to the limo that would take her to the airport—his flight wasn't scheduled to leave for another few hours—it occurred to him that he had gone and done something really stupid.

He had fallen in love with Ivy all over again.

And Ivy had made her position very clear. Her career was the only thing important enough to fill the number one spot in her life right now. She'd worked too hard, for too long, to throw it all away on a man she wasn't sure she trusted.

Well, she hadn't actually said that, but he knew that was what she was thinking.

It was kind of ironic. Ten years ago she'd been ready to settle down and start a life with him, but all he'd wanted was to have fun. To goof off. Now that he was finally ready to slow down and be with her, she had already moved on to bigger and better things.

And if it were his career in jeopardy, he couldn't say for sure that he wouldn't make the same decision.

They had genuine feelings for each other. Their timing was just *way* off.

For some reason that didn't make him feel any better.

The driver put the bags in the trunk, and Dillon opened the door for Ivy. "I had a good time this week."

She set her purse on the seat and turned to him, the car door between them. "Me, too. Do you think Dale will tell anyone he saw us together?"

"I doubt it. And if he does say anything, I'll deny it. Your career is safe."

"Thank you," she said, but instead of sounding relieved, he could swear he heard disappointment in her voice.

The driver got in and started the engine.

"I guess this is it," she said.

Dillon nodded. "I guess it is."

He kept his hands clamped down tightly on the car window, so he wouldn't touch her. Because he knew if he got hold of her again, he might not be able to let go. And that would be a mistake.

It hadn't worked the first time, and they had no guarantees it be any better now. Odds were they would have ended up right where they'd been ten years ago. Divorced and bitter and hating each other. At least this time they were parting as friends.

She had a life, and he had a life, and they were both better off keeping it that way.

"Have a good trip."

"Goodbye." She rose up on her toes and pressed a kiss to his cheek, then she turned and climbed inside the limo. He stood and watched as the limo rolled down the driveway and disappeared around the corner.

It was the second damn time he'd watched that woman walk out of his life.

Ivy had two major problems.

Problem number one was that she was pretty sure her career was officially over.

For the seventh day straight she'd sat at her desk, staring at the computer screen, until her eyes burned with fatigue and strain. Instead of tapping across the keyboard the way they usually did, her hands lay limp and useless in her lap.

Seven days, and she hadn't written a darned word.

What was once so clear to her, so obvious and logical, no longer made sense. The magic was gone. And the explanation was simple. She was a fraud. A charlatan. She'd been giving millions of trusting, naive women lousy advice.

It was humbling and embarrassing to realize that everything she believed in, everything she knew about her life, was a lie. Or at the very least, grossly misconstrued. It was a wrong she needed to right or she feared it would gnaw away at her, little by little, until there was nothing left. Unfortunately, she didn't have the slightest clue how to fix it. What her next move should be.

Which brought her to problem number two. Dillon.

She missed him.

She missed him like she'd never missed anyone before in her life. The first time she'd walked away from him had hurt, but it had also been a relief. The fighting, the heartache—it had been over. All she felt this time was pain and loss. A deep, sharp ache in her chest, as though her heart had been ripped out, filleted, haphazardly sewn back together, then shoved back in the wrong way.

After she'd kissed Dillon goodbye and the limo had set off to the airport, it had taken her exactly three seconds to realize, to admit to herself, that she loved him. The same as the first time, but completely different somehow.

What they'd had back then was thrilling and complicated and volatile. It had burned hot and fast, but what she felt for him now was more mature and undemanding. Simple in its complexity. And deeper than she imagined possible.

They had come full circle, and by letting go the first time, they had somehow grown together. It was finally their time. She was sure, all the way down to her soul, that they could make it work and that they would both be happy.

At least a dozen times she'd opened her mouth to instruct the driver to turn around, to take her back. But she'd been too chicken to do it. How could she willingly destroy her own career? Admit to millions of readers that she was wrong? And how could she not?

But what scared her the most, was what if he rejected her? What if he didn't love her the way she loved him?

What a pathetic excuse for a strong, independent woman she turned out to be.

But damn it, she was sick of playing that role. And the honest truth was, that's all it had been. A role. An act. When she stripped herself down to the core, to the real her, she was still the same old Ivy. Only a little wiser, she hoped.

What it really boiled down to, the thing she had to decide once and for all, was would she rather be successful, or would she rather be happy?

The answer came to her instantly.

Definitely happy.

Well, that wasn't so hard.

And who knows, maybe someday she would be able to manage both. But one thing at a time. First she had to talk to Dillon.

It was a risk. It was possible that he wasn't willing to give her a second chance. He could have moved on by now. But she knew that was a chance she was willing to take. One she had to take.

Oh, my God, she was really going to do this.

She reached for the phone, hand trembling with anticipation. Nothing in her life had ever felt so scary. Or so right.

The instant her hand hit the receiver she realized that she didn't have his number. She could call directory assistance, but she seriously doubted he would be listed.

But she did know where he lived.

Besides, if she was going to grovel, she should at least give him the satisfaction of seeing her face.

She pushed away from her desk. She would go to his house and hope that she was able to get past the front gate. Even if that meant running into his horrible mother. Mrs. Marshall, as Ivy had been instructed to address her, would just have to adjust to having Ivy around again. The same with Ivy's mom. She would have to accept that Dillon had changed. And if she couldn't, if she still believed Ivy was making a mistake, Ivy would just have to learn to tune her out. In fact, she should have learned that a long time ago.

And who knows, maybe a couple of grandchildren to spoil would lighten them both up a little. Right now, she felt as though anything were possible.

She grabbed her keys off the table in the entryway and stuck her feet into one of the pairs of shoes she'd left by the front door. Her hands were shaking and her heart was about to burst from her chest it was beating so hard, but she was determined to see this through.

She turned the knob and swung the door open and— hello!—almost ran face-first into the wall of man standing there.

It took her brain a second or two to process who it was. "Dillon?"

He stood in the hallway outside her apartment, fist raised, as if he'd just been preparing to knock, and he looked just as surprised to see her as she was to see him. Several days' worth of dark, coarse stubble branded his face and his clothes were wrinkled. His hair was a mess and when he slipped off his sunglasses his eyes looked red-rimmed and tired.

Good Lord, he looked about as awful as she felt. For some reason that was a comfort.

He didn't say a word. He just gripped her by her upper arms and tugged her roughly to him. His lips came down hard on hers, rough and sexy and demanding. His beard chafed her chin, fingers dug into her flesh. He tasted like coffee and sex, smelled warm and familiar. Her body went limp and she heard her keys hit the floor.

The kiss was as hot as a flash fire and over just as fast. He set her loose and she stood there, dizzy and disoriented, clutching the door frame to keep from falling over.

Whoa.

If he was trying to knock her off base, he was doing one hell of a job.

He scooped her keys up from the floor. "Going somewhere?"

"Believe it or not, I was just on my way to see you," she said. "We must be on the same wavelength or something."

"No kidding. You were coming to see me?" He looked her up and down, and his brow crinkled. "Like *that*?"

Like what? She looked down at herself and snorted out a laugh. She was still in the baggy pajama bottoms and threadbare T-shirt she'd slept in last night. The sandals on her feet were each a different style and color. Come to think of it, she couldn't remember if she'd even brushed her hair. She hadn't grabbed her purse, either, meaning she didn't have her driver's license. Had she been pulled over, the police might have mistaken her for an escaped lunatic.

"I guess I forgot to get dressed."

"We have to talk," he grumbled. It wasn't a request. It was an order.

"Okay, let's talk."

"Can I come in? If I'm going to grovel, I'm sure as *hell* not going to do it in front of your neighbors."

Grovel?

Dillon laid down the law. He divided and conquered. But Dillon *did not* grovel.

Without waiting for an answer, and in typical Dillon form, he strong-armed his way inside and shut the door behind him.

"Make yourself at home," she mumbled, annoyed, but only a little.

"So here's the deal," he said in that Master of the Universe tone. "I'm not going to let you toss me away again."

So this was his idea of groveling? Ordering her around again?

She crossed her arms over her chest, stuck her chin up in the air. "You're not?"

He settled into an identical, defiant stance. "Nope."

"Do I have a say in this?"

"Nope. I love you, and you love me. Even though you're too damned stubborn to admit it."

Oh, she was, was she? Why in the heck did he think she was coming to see him? To tell him she *didn't* love him?

"For your information, I do love you. Although at times like this I have to wonder why."

"Great, so you won't object to the fact that you're marrying me."

A shiver of excitement scrambled up her spine. He wanted to marry her. "If that was a proposal, you really need to work on your delivery."

"You want me to get down on one knee? Fine." He dropped down in front of her. "How's that?"

"Better." A lot closer to the groveling he'd promised.

He looked her right in the eye and said, "Marry me."

Another demand. For Pete's sake, could he drop the macho act for two seconds?

"What about my work? My career? If we get married, professionally I could be ruined. You said yourself that it was too much to ask me to give up."

The cockiness never wavered. "Too bad. Because I'm asking."

No, he wasn't. He was telling. The way he always did. But knowing how hard it must have been for him to swallow his pride and come here in the first place, this time she didn't mind so much. He was just being Dillon, and she didn't expect him to change. She loved him, warts and all. This time she was going into the deal with her eyes wide open.

That didn't mean it wouldn't be entertaining to mess with him just a little. "And if I say no?"

"You won't."

"But what if I do?"

He blew out an exasperated breath. "I'll ask again. And again. And I'll keep asking until you say yes."

The odds of a normal, traditional proposal seemed to hover somewhere in the million-to-one range. "Well, then, I guess I don't have much of a choice. I guess I have to say yes."

He rose to his feet and pulled her to him, not so roughly this time, and kissed her again. This time it lasted longer, felt…sweeter. Tender, even. His hands cupped her face, lips brushing lazily back and forth across hers. She heard him sigh, felt him shudder with satisfaction.

The kiss trailed off slowly, his lips lingering above hers. And when she opened her eyes to look at him, he was smiling that lazy, happy smile.

"This could be complicated," she warned him.

He only shrugged. "We'll figure it out."

"Our mothers—"

"—will adjust," he finished for her. He glanced over her shoulder, down the hall. "Have you got a bedroom in this place?"

"I want kids," she warned him.

"Great." He lowered his head, nibbled the curve of her neck. A new round of shivers exploded across her skin.

"I'm serious, Dillon."

"Fine with me." He licked the shell of her ear, nipped at it with his teeth. Desire ignited in the pit of her belly and burned its way through her arms and legs and into her head.

"I want at least two," she told him, her voice coming

out breathy and soft. "And I want to do it soon, before I'm too old."

"Good idea." He walked her backward down the hall, his hands gentle yet determined as they circled her waist, easing her T-shirt up. "In fact, I think we should start trying right now."

Apparently she wasn't moving quickly enough, because he lifted her right off her feet and carried her the rest of the way.

He found the bedroom on the first try and shouldered his way through the door, then he all but tossed her on the bed and dropped down beside her. Instead of ravaging her, the way she expected, he just looked down at her and smiled.

"This is going to be good." He kissed her forehead, the tip of her nose. "This is going to be really good."

"Yes," she agreed, "it is." They really had come full circle, and wound up exactly where they were supposed to be. She wasn't going to try to fool herself into thinking it would be easy. They were still both stubborn as hell. But this time, at least, they had maturity on their side.

"You know we're going to have to work at this," she said, and he nodded solemnly.

"I know."

"We're going to have to keep the lines of communication open or we'll end up just like we were ten years ago."

"I understand that."

"You can't just—"

He silenced her with a kiss. A long, slow, mind-melting deep one.

When it was over, she felt hot and fuzzy-headed. "What was I saying?"

"Ivy, you don't have to worry. We'll do what we have to do. Whatever it takes." His eyes searched her face, filled with love and affection and respect. "I let you go twice, darlin'. That's a mistake I won't be making again."

Coming soon from Series Press—from half the author team who brought us the bestselling self-help book The Modern Woman's Guide to Divorce (And the Joy of Staying Single), Not All Men Are Pigs or What Was I Thinking?

Mediterranean Nights

Join the guests and crew of Alexandra's Dream,
*the newest luxury ship to set sail on the
romantic Mediterranean, as they experience
the glamorous world of cruising.*

*A new Harlequin continuity series
begins in June 2007 with*
FROM RUSSIA, WITH LOVE
by Ingrid Weaver.

*Marina Artamova books a cabin on the
luxurious cruise ship* Alexandra's Dream, *when
she finds out that her orphaned nephew and
his adoptive father are aboard. She's determined
to be reunited with the boy...but the romantic
ambience of the ship and her undeniable
attraction to a man she considers her enemy
are about to interfere with her quest!*

Turn the page for a sneak preview!

Piraeus, Greece

"THERE SHE IS, Stefan. Alexandra's Dream." David Anderson squatted beside his new son and pointed at the dark blue hull that towered above the pier. The cruise ship was a majestic sight, twelve decks high and as long as a city block. A circle of silver and gold stars, the logo of the Liberty Cruise Line, gleamed from the swept-back smokestack. Like some legendary sea creature born for the water, the ship emanated power from every sleek curve—even at rest it held the promise of motion. "That's going to be our home for the next ten days."

The child beside him remained silent, his cheeks working in and out as he sucked furiously on his thumb. Hair so blond it appeared white ruffled against his forehead in the harbor breeze. The baby-sweet scent unique to the very young mingled with the tang of the sea.

"Ship," David said. "Uh, *parakhod.*"

From beneath his bangs, Stefan looked at *Alexandra's Dream.* Although he didn't release his thumb, the corners of his mouth tightened with the beginning of a smile.

David grinned. That was Stefan's first smile this afternoon, one of only two since they had left the orphanage yesterday. It was probably because of the boat—according to the orphanage staff, the boy loved boats, which was the main reason David had decided to book this cruise. Then again, there was a strong possibility the smile could have been a reaction to David's attempt at pocket-dictionary Russian. Whatever the cause, it was a good start.

The liaison from the adoption agency had claimed that Stefan had been taught some English, but David had yet to see evidence of it. David continued to speak, positive his son would understand his tone even if he couldn't grasp the words. "This is her maiden voyage. Her first trip, just like this is our first trip, and that makes it special." He motioned toward the stage that had been set up on the pier beneath the ship's bow. "That's why everyone's celebrating."

The ship's official christening ceremony had been held the day before and had been a closed affair, with only the cruise-line executives and VIP guests invited, but the stage hadn't yet been disassembled. Banners bearing the blue and white of the Greek flag of the ship's owner, as well as the Liberty circle of stars logo, draped the edges of the platform. In the center, a group of musicians and a dance troupe dressed in traditional white folk costumes performed for the benefit of *Alexandra's Dream*'s first passengers. Their audience was in a festive mood, snapping their fingers in time to the music while the dancers twirled and wove through their steps.

David bobbed his head to the rhythm of the mandolins. They were playing a folk tune that seemed vaguely familiar, possibly from a movie he'd seen. He hummed a few notes. "Catchy melody, isn't it?"

Stefan turned his gaze on David. His eyes were a striking shade of blue, as cool and pale as a winter horizon and far too solemn for a child not yet five. Still, the smile that hovered at the corners of his mouth persisted. He moved his head with the music, mirroring David's motion.

David gave a silent cheer at the interaction. Hopefully, this cruise would provide countless opportunities for more. "Hey, good for you," he said. "Do you like the music?"

The child's eyes sparked. He withdrew his thumb with a pop. *"Moozika!"*

"Music. Right!" David held out his hand. "Come on, let's go closer so we can watch the dancers."

Stefan grasped David's hand quickly, as if he feared it would be withdrawn. In an instant his budding smile was replaced by a look close to panic.

Did he remember the car accident that had killed his parents? It would be a mercy if he didn't. As far as David knew, Stefan had never spoken of it to anyone. Whatever he had seen had made him run so far from the crash that the police hadn't found him until the next day. The event had traumatized him to the extent that he hadn't uttered a word until his fifth week at the orphanage. Even now he seldom talked.

David sat back on his heels and brushed the hair from Stefan's forehead. That solemn, too-old gaze locked with his, and for an instant, David felt as if he looked back in time at an image of himself thirty years ago.

He didn't need to speak the same language to understand exactly how this boy felt. He knew what it meant to be alone and powerless among strangers, trying to be brave and tough but wishing with every fiber of his being for a place to belong, to be safe, and most of all for someone to love him....

He knew in his heart he would be a good parent to Stefan. It was why he had never considered halting the adoption process after Ellie had left him. He hadn't balked when he'd learned of the recent claim by Stefan's spinster aunt, either; the absentee relative had shown up too late for her case to be considered. The adoption was meant to be. He and this child already shared a bond that went deeper than paperwork or legalities.

A seagull screeched overhead, making Stefan start and press closer to David.

"That's my boy," David murmured. He swallowed hard, struck by the simple truth of what he had just said. *That's* my *boy*.

"I CAN'T BE PATIENT, RUDOLPH. I'm not going to stand by and watch my nephew get ripped from his country and his roots to live on the other side of the world."

Rudolph hissed out a slow breath. "Marina, I don't like the sound of that. What are you planning?"

"I'm going to talk some sense into this American kidnapper."

"No. Absolutely not. No offence, but diplomacy is not your strong suit."

"Diplomacy be damned. Their ship's due to sail at five o'clock."

"Then you wouldn't have an opportunity to speak with him even if his lawyer agreed to a meeting."

"I'll have ten days of opportunities, Rudolph, since I plan to be on board that ship."

* * * * *

*Follow Marina and David as they
join forces to uncover the reason behind
little Stefan's unusual silence, and the
secret behind the death of his parents....*

Look for From Russia, With Love
*by Ingrid Weaver
in stores June 2007.*

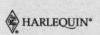

Mediterranean
N I G H T S ™

Tycoon Elias Stamos is launching his newest luxury cruise ship from his home port in Greece. But someone from his past is eager to expose old secrets and to see the Stamos empire crumble.

Mediterranean Nights
launches in June 2007 with...

FROM RUSSIA, WITH LOVE
by *Ingrid Weaver*

Join the guests and crew of *Alexandra's Dream* as they are drawn into a world of glamour, romance and intrigue in this new 12-book series.

HARLEQUIN®

///// **NASCAR**

In February...

Collect all 4 debut novels in
the Harlequin NASCAR series.

SPEED DATING
by *USA TODAY* bestselling author
Nancy Warren

THUNDERSTRUCK
by Roxanne St. Claire

HEARTS UNDER CAUTION
by Gina Wilkins

DANGER ZONE
by Debra Webb

*On sale
February
2007*

And in May don't miss...

Gabby, a gutsy female NASCAR driver,
can't believe her mother is harping at her
again. How many times does she have
to say it? She's not going to help run the
family's corporation. She's not shopping
for a husband of the right pedigree. And
there's no way she's giving up racing!

SPEED BUMPS *is one of four
exciting Harlequin NASCAR books that
will go on sale in May.*

SEE COUPON INSIDE.

www.GetYourHeartRacing.com   NASCARMAY

HARLEQUIN®
Super Romance®

Acclaimed author
Brenda Novak
returns to Dundee, Idaho, with

COULDA BEEN A COWBOY

After gaining custody of his infant son,
professional athlete Tyson Garnier hopes to escape
the media and find some privacy in Dundee, Idaho.
He also finds Dakota Brown. But is she ready for the
potential drama that comes with him?

Also watch for:

BLAME IT ON THE DOG by Amy Frazier
(Singles...with Kids)

HIS PERFECT WOMAN by Kay Stockham

DAD FOR LIFE by Helen Brenna
(A Little Secret)

MR. IRRESISTIBLE by Karina Bliss

WANTED MAN by Ellen K. Hartman

Available June 2007 wherever Harlequin books are sold!

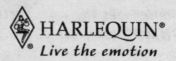

HARLEQUIN®
Live the emotion

SPECIAL EDITION™

COMING IN JUNE

HER LAST FIRST DATE

by *USA TODAY* bestselling author
SUSAN MALLERY

After one too many bad dates, Crissy Phillips
finally swore off men. Recently widowed,
pediatrician Josh Daniels can't risk losing his
heart. With an intense attraction pulling them
together, will their fear keep them apart?
Or will one wild night change everything…?

positively +pregnant

Sometimes the unexpected
is the best news of all….

REQUEST YOUR FREE BOOKS!

2 FREE NOVELS
PLUS 2
FREE GIFTS!

Silhouette®

Passionate, Powerful, Provocative!

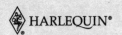

HARLEQUIN®

American ROMANCE®

**is proud to present a special treat this
Fourth of July with three stories
to kick off your summer!**

SUMMER LOVIN'
by
Marin Thomas,
Laura Marie Altom
Ann Roth

This year, celebrating the Fourth of July in Silver Cliff,
Colorado, is going to be special. There's an all-year
high school reunion taking place before the old
school building gets torn down. As old flames find
each other and new romances begin, this small
town is looking like the perfect place
for some summer lovin'!

*Available June 2007
wherever Harlequin books are sold.*

www.eHarlequin.com HAR75169

COMING NEXT MONTH

#1801 FORTUNE'S FORBIDDEN WOMAN—Heidi Betts
Dakota Fortunes
Can he risk the family honor to fulfill an unrequited passion with the one woman he's forbidden to have?

#1802 SIX-MONTH MISTRESS—Katherine Garbera
The Mistresses
She was contracted to be his mistress in exchange for his help in getting her struggling business off the ground. Now he's come to collect his prize.

#1803 AN IMPROPER AFFAIR—Anna DePalo
Millionaire of the Month
This ruthless businessman is on the verge of extracting the ultimate revenge…until he falls for the woman who could jeopardize his entire plan.

#1804 THE MILLIONAIRE'S INDECENT PROPOSAL— Emilie Rose
Monte Carlo Affairs
When an attractive stranger offers her a million euros to become his mistress, will she prove his theory that everyone has a price?

#1805 BETWEEN THE CEO'S SHEETS—Charlene Sands
She'd been paid off to leave him. Now he wants revenge and will stop at nothing until he settles the score…and gets her back in his bed.

#1806 RICH MAN'S REVENGE—Tessa Radley
He'd marry his enemy's daughter and extract his long-denied revenge—but his new bride has her own plan for him.

SDCNM0507